Published in Nashville, Tennessee by Tommy Nelson™, a division of Thomas Nelson, Inc.

Scripture quotations are from the *International Children's Bible®, New Century Version®:* Copyright © 1986, 1988, 1999 by Tommy Nelson™, a division of Thomas Nelson, Inc.

Creative director: Robin Crouch
Series consultant: Dandi Daley Mackall
Computer programming consultant: Lucinda C. Thurman

Library of Congress Cataloging-in-Publication Data

Mackall, Dandi Daley.
   Portrait of Lies/written by Dandi Daley Mackall ; created by Terry Brown.
      p. cm. – (TodaysGirls.com ; 2)
   Summary: Encouraged by her close friends and a mystery supporter in cyberspace, Jamie decides to enter a contest to win an art camp scholarship despite her own lack of confidence in her artistic ability.
   ISBN 0-8499-7561-1
   [1. Artists—Fiction. 2. Friendship—Fiction. 3. Christian life—Fiction.] I. Brown, Terry, 1961 – II. Title. III. Series.
PZ7.M1905 Po 2000
[Fic]—dc21   00-020021
                                                                      CIP

Printed in the United States of America
00 01 02 03 04 05 QBV 0 9 8 7 6 5 4 3 2 1

PORTRAIT OF LIES

WRITTEN BY
Dandi Daley Mackall

CREATED BY
Terry K. Brown

Tommy
NELSON™
Thomas Nelson, Inc.
Nashville

Web Words

2 to/too

4 for

ACK! disgusted

A/S/L age/sex/location

B4 before

BBL be back later

BBS be back soon

BF boyfriend

BRB be right back

CU see you

Cuz because

CYAL8R see you later

Dunno don't know

Enuf enough

FYI for your information

G2G or **GTG** I've got to go

GF girlfriend

GR8 great

H&K hug and kiss

IC I see

IN2 into

IRL in real life

JLY Jesus loves you

JK just kidding

JMO just my opinion

K okay

Kewl cool

KOTC kiss on the cheek

LOL laugh out loud

LTNC long time no see

LY love you

L8R later

NBD no big deal

NU new/knew

NW no way

OIC oh, I see

QT cutie

RO rock on

ROFL rolling on floor laughing

RU are you

SOL sooner or later

Splain explain

SWAK sealed with a kiss

SYS see you soon

Thanx (or) **thx** thanks

TNT till next time

TTFN ta ta for now

TTYL talk to you later

U you

U NO you know

UD you'd (you would)

UR your/you're/you are

WB welcome back

WBS write back soon

WTG way to go

Y why

(Note: Remember that capitalization may vary.)

iv

chapter.1

J amie!" Bren whined. "We're missing out! Click out of search! Everybody's already in our chat room!"

"Uh huh." Jamie barely listened to her best friend, too caught up in the list of schools scrolling down her computer screen.

"Minnesota School of the Arts." Jamie read the computer entry aloud. She'd been squinting at the blue screen for so long that her eyes hurt. "I've never heard of that one, Bren. Think they're big enough to have a summer program for young artists?" *And to have plenty of scholarships,* she wondered. Getting into an exclusive summer art camp would be her first step toward becoming a real artist.

Bren peered over Jamie's shoulder as pictures of the campus took shape. "Jamie," Bren said, "why would anyone go to Minnesota on purpose? Dad had a medical convention in Minneapolis once and came home with a million mosquito bites. You know their license plates say, 'Land of 10,000 Lakes?' They should say, 'Land of a Million Mosquitoes.'"

Jamie shook her head and went back to the other art schools.

"Jamie, look!" Bren screamed in Jamie's ear as the blinking e-mail alert appeared.

YOU'VE GOT MAIL

"Aren't you going to click it?" asked Bren. "You can't just leave it there!"

"In a minute, Bren." Jamie kept scrolling down the long list of art schools. "Oklahoma, nope. Arizona, maybe . . . "

"This is too much!" Bren cried. "It is un-American not to get your e-mail! No kidding, Jamie. Scientists have discovered it's not healthy to leave your mailbox full. It makes you repressed or depressed or something. And it gives you wrinkles! Do you want wrinkles??"

Jamie let Bren babble. "New Mexico, Montana . . ."

"Jamie Chandler, it is against the law not to check your e-mail! A federal offense—mail tampering. And I'm positive the Supreme Court will back me up on this!"

"Alright. You win." Jamie clicked *yes* to read her e-mail. The mailbox came up with one new message, a cyber ad: Special hot deals on flights to Morocco and Madrid!

"Good thing we checked that one out, huh, Bren?" Jamie said, clicking out of e-mail and back to her art school search. "Iowa, Nebraska, Kansas . . . "

"Ew! Kansas!" Bren squealed, pointing to a list at the top of the screen for Kansas State International Art Fest. "They should have license plates that say, 'We're flat.' No, no—I've got it. They could say, 'Toto, we're not in Indiana anymore.'

"You know my dad drove us to Yellowstone one year, and we had to drive through Kansas, which I thought might be cool, since I love the *Wizard of Oz* so much, but it turned out to be the longest state in the whole world, with the fewest fast food places!"

Jamie had to grin. Bren Mickler had been her best friend for as long as Jamie could remember, but her friend would never understand. Bren had no idea what it felt like to really want something. As soon as Bren wanted anything, her parents ran out and bought it for her—that day! Bren's dad was so wealthy he could—and would—send his daughter, his only daughter, to any school in the entire world.

"Look at this one, Bren!" Jamie clicked on Maine Artist's Colony. "That's exactly the kind of program I want," she said, imagining what it would be like to do nothing except draw and paint for a whole month. No school, no little sisters, no waiting tables.

Bren pulled a Milky Way out of her gym bag and broke off a piece. "Maine? Now they've got cute little lobsters all over their license plates. You know what they do with their lobsters, don't you? I say, Maine plates should read: 'See these animals? We drop them in boiling water while they're still kicking.'

"I knew this guy once. Well, I didn't actually know him. I met him at swim camp. Amber and Maya were there, too. Anyway, he was so stuck up! Maya beat him in the butterfly. And he had this accent—"

"Bren! Could we focus on me for one minute, please?"

Jamie watched Bren's golden-brown eyes open as wide as quarters. Her hand hung suspended, fingers pinching a piece of chocolate, ready to pop it like popcorn between neatly lipsticked lips.

"I'm sorry, Bren," Jamie said, leaning back in the kitchen chair she always had to swipe for the computer when Bren came over. At Bren's house, computers got their own chairs. "It's just that right now I don't have one piece of art good enough to put into a portfolio. And I need everything—portraits, stills, water-colors, acrylics, oils, ceramics. And not the stuff we make in Mrs. Woolsey's class either."

Bren feigned shock. "What? You mean you can't use tooth-pick towers or Popsicle-stick pictures?"

"It's not funny, Bren," Jamie griped, nervously circling her worn-out mouse on its pad. "If I don't have an awesome portfo-lio to show, I won't get a scholarship to a good art college."

"Excuse me?" Bren said. "I must have mistaken you for the Jamie Chandler who's only a sophomore in *high school.* I don't even want to think about college. Dad does enough of that for both of us! All he wants to do is visit this school or that univer-sity, as if I didn't have a life on the weekends. He and Mom argue all the time—OK, not argue, *discuss*—because Mom wants me to stay in Indiana. I don't care where I end up, as long as I end up becoming a famous fashion designer."

She would, too. Jamie studied Bren's perfect look—her earrings (emeralds in top holes, gold studs below), the chain around Bren's neck that probably cost more than Jamie's mom made in a month as a paralegal. She wore exactly the right cropped jeans and designer shirt, and she had her thick, brown hair styled in a smooth, straight cut by a hairstylist in the city.

But it was more than that. Bren was magnetic. Without even trying, Bren could look like fashion models on TV, laugh like women in romantic movies, and set half of the trends in school just by wearing or doing what she wanted. Single-handedly, Bren had started a judo fad, ushered in a high-topped sneaker craze, and launched revivals of the tango, head scarves, and even Hula-Hoops.

Jamie, on the other hand, had never followed a fad, much less led one. A full three inches shorter than Bren's 5'7", Jamie kept her light-blonde hair a little long—not by design, but because she could brush it back in a ponytail in two seconds flat. That was all the time she had on school mornings with three other females and one bathroom in the house. Sometimes Jamie wondered why Bren was friends with her.

Jamie kept moving through cyberspace, hopping from Web site to Web site. She knew she was lucky they had a computer. It was a miracle her mom, despite loud protests from Jamie's sisters, had agreed to keep it in Jamie's room "for the time being." But she couldn't help wishing this computer were as fast as Bren's. She'd have been done by now if they'd been at Bren's.

Jamie let go of the mouse. Something on the screen shouted at her, as if all along it had been waiting for her, hoping Jamie Chandler would end up on this page. Bren was chattering on about some guy she was trying to get to notice her, but Jamie shut out everything except the words on the screen, words that could change her whole life.

She read the entry out loud. "'Interlochen Arts Camp—Now seeking aspiring artists from across the U.S. to share the Interlochen experience—Interlochen Center for the Arts, Interlochen, Michigan.'"

"Aspiring artists?" Bren repeated. "Jamie, that's you! You're an artist! You're aspiring! And Michigan, the UP!"

Trancelike, Jamie continued: "'Selected high school undergraduates spend July 2–30 on the Interlochen campus, under the mentoring of professional artists, as well as university professors. The goal is to help talented students develop a portfolio that will help them get college scholarships.'"

It was as if this Web site had read Jamie's mind, eavesdropped on her dreams. Jamie knew that an art scholarship was the only way she'd get into a good school. Her mom worked ten hours a day just to keep the three of them fed and in Levi's.

"It's perfect, Jamie!" Bren insisted. "Do it! I can't even think of a bad license plate slogan for Michigan. I knew a guy from Marquette once, and he . . ."

But Jamie wasn't listening. She read every word on the screen in front of her—all about classes in charcoal sketching, portrait painting, still lifes, ceramics, mixed media. She drank in the descriptions of spacious, private rooms and meals in the prize-winning cafeteria.

At the very bottom of the screen was a form to fill out. And just above that, in small gray numbers, was a list of fees and expenses. "Two thousand dollars?" Jamie heard her voice come out as a whisper, but inside it was a scream. *Two thousand dol-lars!* Her chair tipped over and crashed to the floor. Suddenly realizing she was on her feet, nose practically pressed to the computer screen, Jamie pulled her chair back up and plopped down in it. "Two thousand dollars? It might as well cost two *million* dollars, Bren."

"Don't give up!" Bren scolded, scooting her chair closer to the keyboard. "Maybe they have scholarships or something." Bren clicked back to the home page, then clicked again and again. "Yes!" she shouted. "Jamie, look at this! They have a contest!"

Jamie sat up fast. "What kind of a contest?"

"It says, 'Entries must be posted by October 1.'" Bren growled at the computer. "This thing is so slow, Jamie!"

Jamie tried to keep herself from getting too excited. A contest. The idea of competing scared her. And the deadline was just a lit-tle over a week away. But if they wanted watercolors, she had one of a field of dandelions that wasn't all that bad. She'd worked all summer on a couple of pieces of ceramic art. Maybe . . .

"Here it is!" Bren said. "Portrait contest! Scan your best portrait work in any medium and send to their e-mail address."

Portrait? Jamie had heard the expression "sinking heart" before, but this was the first time she had experienced it. She felt the disappointment like a lead ball dropping through her chest. "I don't have anything to send," she said softly. "I haven't done a portrait since seventh grade." She let out a sigh. "Even if I had, it wouldn't be good enough to win a contest."

"Don't say that, Jamie! You're great! You're the best!" Bren sounded like she was giving one of her cheerleading cheers. Jamie half-expected her to break out with a chorus of "Give me a *J!* Give me an *A!* . . ."

"Just try it, Jamie. Do a portrait! You have a whole week. That's plenty of time."

At the word *time*, Bren's body stiffened. "Time!" she exclaimed, exiting the art school Web site and typing in TodaysGirls.com. "It's after five, Jamie! We have to go to the Web site. Bet Amber and Maya are already waiting for us."

Jamie couldn't think of anything but the contest. She imagined aspiring artists all over the nation at that very moment putting the finishing touches on their masterpieces, beautiful portraits they had taken months to create under the admiring eyes of their mentors. How could she compete with that?

Bren was already punching in her password on the girls' site.

Welcome to TodaysGirls.com
password: Bren004

Forming their own site with a chat room had been Amber's idea. They'd been squeezing into other chat rooms online, but they usually ended up creating private rooms to avoid freaks who obviously couldn't get enough attention in the real world. Amber and Maya were juniors and had done most of the work getting the Web site up and running. But Bren and Jamie—and even Maya's little sister Morgan—did their share in maintaining it. Jamie ran the Artist's Corner, where any of the girls could post artwork.

The Thought for the Day popped up—Amber's responsibility:

> **Depend on the Lord. Trust him, and he will take care of you.–Psalm 37:5. Try it! Having trouble with that English lit paper or that calculus problem? Pray about it–but don't forget to do your homework!**

"I don't know where Amber comes up with this stuff, do you, Jamie?" Bren asked, clicking on the *chat* icon.

Jamie reread Amber's daily thought still showing at the top of the screen. She wished she could trust God to come up with the money she'd need for summer art camp. If she could get the two thousand, maybe she could still get into the Interlochen program. But what if God didn't want her to go? What if God didn't even want her to be an artist?

Bren had already jumped into the flow of cyber chat. She typed in the dialog box:

> chicChick: nu u'd be here!
> faithful1: GDM8s.

"Amber says, 'Good day, mates,'" Bren said out loud. Bren probably logged in ten times more than Jamie did in the chat room, but then Bren probably spent a hundred times more hours than Jamie chatting in person, on the phone, or in any other conceivable mode of communication. And sometimes Jamie liked to try other chat rooms where no one knew her.

Bren kept up her end of the dialog:

> chicChick: GR8 site! it looks so kewl! :)
> faithful1: GR8 haven't been here long. Dad left again. I
>   think he'll be gone for two weeks. he'll miss the art
>   show! : (

It was hard for Jamie to feel too sorry for Amber. True, her dad did travel a lot. But he owned the trucking company he sometimes drove for. And at least Amber had a father. Jamie could hardly remember what her father looked like. He'd walked out on them when she was five and Mom was still pregnant with

Jessica. Not that Jamie cared. They didn't need him anyway.

She read over Bren's shoulder as her slender fingers input her next message:

> **chicChick: rembrandt's been art school hunting. only has a couple more years of high school, u no?**
> **faithful1: good 4 her! I've been checking out creative writing departments at Purdue, FWIW. dad's checking out law schools. : (**
> **chicChick: i hear that!**

Jamie reached over and typed her own message.

> **rembrandt: i'm just trying to find a great art camp or workshop i can do this summer. No biggie.**

Of course, it was a big deal. Jamie just didn't want everybody feeling sorry for her. Finding a great art camp wasn't the problem. But finding the money to go to one was.

> **faithful1: has rembrandt checked out any art contests on the web?**

"Tell her I don't have anything to compete with," Jamie told Bren. "Never mind. Let me do it." Jamie reached in front of Bren to type:

rembrandt: me win a contest? LOL! i don't have anything good enough.
faithful1: rembrandt, u r GR8! u should enter and win!
rembrandt: NW.

Bren elbowed Jamie away from the screen. "Jamie," she said. "Don't say 'no way'! Amber's right! Maybe we can help." She waited for her dialog to appear in the box. "Your computer is so slow, Jamie! You ought to get a new one!"

Just like that? Jamie thought. *If I were Bren, maybe.*

Before Bren could finish typing her message, a new name entered the room:

nycbutterfly: rembrandt, r u still here? thought you
   would be at the Gnosh.

The Gnosh Pit! "Maya's right!" Jamie cried, shooting out of her chair. She ran to her bedroom door, remembered her shoes, and scurried back to look for them. "I have to get to work! I want to ask Maya's dad for an advance and more hours. I can't be late! And I haven't even fed Jordan and Jessica yet."

"You make them sound like dogs instead of sisters," Bren said, not looking up from the keyboard.

"They might as well be," Jamie said, hunting for her other tennis shoe. She dropped to her knees to look under the bed. "If I don't feed my darling little sisters, they'll bite my head off."

The missing shoe lay on its side, half-hidden by socks and dust bunnies. She dragged it out by its laces. Something about the room suddenly felt wrong, foreboding, as if they were suspended in the seconds between the flash of lightning and the boom of thunder.

"That smell," she muttered, focusing on a weird odor coming through the heat vents. "What's that smell?"

"Mmmm, FO? Foot odor?" Bren offered, without looking away from the screen.

"Not that!" Jamie said. The stench got stronger—a familiar smell that made her feel like her stomach was rebooting.

From way down the hall came a loud, spine-rattling scream. It reached Jamie at the exact second she identified the odor: smoke!

chapter.2

"Smoke!" Jamie shrieked, jerking her bedroom door open and racing down the hall.

"Fire?" Bren cried right behind her. "Jamie, is it roll, drop, stop? Or roll, stop, drop? Or—"

The smoke alarm buzzed and buzzed. Smoke grew thicker.

"Jessica! Jordan! Where are you?"

Jamie heard coughing. "Here! We're in here!" Jessica's voice came from the kitchen.

"Bren!" Jamie shouted, unable to see through all the smoke. "Go call 911! I'm going in for my sisters!"

"Be careful!" Bren's shout faded into a cough.

"I'm coming, Jessica!" Jamie yelled, her eyes burning as a gray cloud of smoke billowed around her. She shut her eyes, dropped to all fours, and burst into the kitchen on hands and knees. "Where's Jordan?"

"Shut that stupid alarm off!" Jordan didn't sound scared. She sounded angry.

"Jordan, are you OK?" Jamie opened her eyes. Her sisters were waving their arms, fanning away smoke. Jamie got to her feet. "We have to get out of here!" she said. But even as she said it, she felt adrenaline drain from her veins.

"Just turn off that alarm!" Jordan insisted. At twelve, Jordan was almost as tall as Jamie, and she was much more commanding. People listened to Jordan Chandler.

"I'll get it," Jessica said, dragging the kitchen stool to the hallway.

"What's—" Jamie stopped. The smoke had cleared to a low-lying cloud, and now she could see what her sister was holding—a big saucepan full of black charcoal. "Jordan!" she screamed. "What on earth do you think you're doing?"

Jordan twisted her lips into a smart-alecky grin and held out the disgusting pan to her sister. "Want some macaroni?"

"You—how—?" Jamie felt as if her throat had caught fire and wouldn't let her words out. She took a deep breath, then coughed. "It was a macaroni fire?" she managed.

"And cheese," Jordan said matter-of-factly, as if she hadn't almost burned down their kitchen. "Personally, I think it was the cheese."

The alarm shut off, but Jamie's head was still buzzing. "How can anybody—even you—burn macaroni?"

"And cheese," Jordan said. "Besides, if you'd been doing what you were supposed to do, none of this would have happened. But no! You just had to play on the computer. What was I supposed to do? Starve?"

"I have a job!" Jamie protested. "And school! And chores! And I would have gotten dinner if you could—!"

"Stop it. Please?" Jessica's soft, pleading voice was probably the only thing that could have stopped Jamie. "Don't fight, OK? Jordan didn't mean to do it. She was trying to help."

"Yeah!" Jordan seconded, dropping the blackened pan into the sink with a loud clang. It sizzled and sent smoke straight up in a puff that smelled like the old steel factory Jamie used to bike past at the edge of town. "I couldn't wait all day! You were hogging the Internet. And I have friends to call."

"That's no excuse for nearly—" Jamie started.

"Please, Jamie? It was my fault, too. I was hungry. Jordan and I will clean it up before Mom gets home. Don't be mad." Jessica's eyes were watering. Unlike her sisters and mother, Jess had black hair and small green eyes that seemed to look right through you. Mom called her the world's best nine-year-old peacemaker.

Jamie melted. She bent down and hugged Jessica. "It's OK, Jess. Sorry I got crazy. It's over now."

A faint, weird, high-pitched sound registered somewhere in Jamie's brain. It grew louder and louder. Sirens!

"Bren called 911!" Jamie said, remembering now. "Those are fire trucks! They're coming here!" Jamie ran to the living room and looked out the picture window. Three fire trucks pulled up on their lawn, right over Mom's mums. Bren stood in the yard, yelling and waving them in.

"Way to go, Jamie!" Jordan said.

Jamie raced to the door and almost ran into a fireman. The man grabbed her around the waist and lifted her off the ground.

"It's alright!" he said. "We'll get you out! Any more inside?"

Jamie couldn't speak. Three more firemen pushed past them, pulling a huge, flat hose.

"Let me down!" Jordan cried. "Get out of our house!"

"In here!" yelled the leader of the hose brigade, racing to the kitchen.

"No!" Jamie cried. She was plopped down outside, one foot in the pansies.

Jordan and Jessica came out, one on each shoulder of the biggest man Jamie had ever seen.

"Stop!" Jamie yelled. "Put my sisters down!" The fire hose continued to snake inside, pulled faster and faster. "Don't turn on the water! The fire's already out!"

But no one would listen to her. Jamie watched helplessly as the firefighters disappeared into the house.

"Are you OK?" Bren grabbed all three girls in a group hug. "I did it! I actually called 911 and remembered your address and told them your house was on fire and waited like they said until they got here! This is so exciting! I hope your computer didn't burn down. Is everybody OK? Somebody's here from Channel 7 news! Are you sure nobody got hurt?"

"Only our macaroni," Jessica said.

"And cheese," added Jordan.

Jess filled Bren in while Jamie tried to find a fireman who would listen to her. Seconds later, the firemen stomped out of the house, hose in hand, water off. "All clear!" said the fireman who had grabbed Jamie.

Another firefighter walked up. "Is this your house?" she asked.

Jamie nodded. Actually, they rented the house, but she didn't think the firewoman really cared.

"Where are your parents?"

Before Jamie could get out her answer, she heard her mom's frantic shouts behind them.

"I can't believe it!" she cried. "Girls! Are you alright?"

Jamie ran to her mother, who already had Jessica and Jordan in her arms. "I was so worried!" Mom said, tears streaking her makeup. "Mrs. Hines called. I got here as soon as I could."

"I was the one who called 911 from Mrs. Hines's house!" Bren said proudly.

They all talked at once until Mom calmed down and the fire trucks drove off, and the spectators dispersed, and the Channel 7 people left disappointed.

Bren stared longingly after the departing cameraman. "They

say everybody gets fifteen minutes of fame. I guess all we got was fifteen minutes of flame." She pivoted back to them. "But you're all fine! And that's what counts! I think that after everything Jordan and Jessica have been through, they should be able to have chocolate ice cream for dinner and brownies for dessert."

"You are so cool, Bren," Jordan said. "Why don't you be our sister instead of Jamie?"

"I'd like both of you to be our sisters," Jessica said, her furrowed brow making her look a little like Grandma Couch.

"Shoot!" Jamie said, remembering her job. "Now I'll really be late to work!" How could she ask Mr. Cross for an advance for art camp if she showed up late for work?

"I can drive you," Mom offered, glancing around as if she couldn't remember where she'd left the car. She ran her fingers through her short blonde hair.

"That's OK. I can make it faster on foot," Jamie said.

"Oh right," Jordan complained. "Leave us with the mess."

Jamie took off at a dead run. "Later!" she hollered back. "Love you!"

She waved to Mrs. Hines as she took the shortcut through her yard and over her fence. She skirted the park and jogged the rest of the way to the Gnosh Pit. Jamie was gasping for breath as she flew through the front door of the restaurant. The door swung back hard and smashed into something.

"Ow!"

Or somebody.

"I am so sorry!" Jamie said, pulling the door back to see who she'd creamed into the wall. "I was late and I didn't think—" Jamie stopped, horrified. It was Mark Wellington, a guy from art class. She could have died on the spot. Let them erect a monument to her right there: Gnosh Pit server fell over dead here.

Mark rubbed his nose. His glasses hung crooked. A lock of thick brown hair hung over one eye. "I—I was just checking out the poster," he stammered.

The poster, a Miró abstract, was Jamie's attempt to bring a little class to the Gnosh Pit—not that the place was that bad. Maya's dad had a thing about the fifties. All the booths and tables were outlined in chrome, with old car parts and fake neon signs on the walls. After a fuss, Mr. Cross had agreed to let Jamie hang the abstract . . . behind the door.

"You're bleeding!" Jamie cried. Blood trickled from Mark's nose. He cupped his hand under his nostrils to catch it. Jamie pulled out a wad of napkins from the nearest table and pushed them at Mark's nose.

"Ow!" he cried, backing away from her. His head bonked the wall. His hand flew instinctively to his head, where he unwittingly rubbed blood into his hair. Red drops splattered the floor, and napkins flew everywhere.

Jamie heard herself saying over and over, "I am so sorry! I am so sorry!"

Mr. Cross ran up to them. "What's going on—? Oh, my word! What happened to you? Where did this blood come from?"

Jamie grabbed another handful of napkins. She dropped to her knees and wiped up the little drops of red at their feet.

Mr. Cross sniffed the air. *Sniff sniff!* "What's that—*sniff sniff*—smell? That's smoke! I smell smoke! Where is it coming from?"

Jamie, still on her knees, said, "Um, that . . . that would be me, Mr. Cross."

"You?" he shouted. "That would be you?" Joseph Cross, hands on his hips, nostrils flared, stared down at Jamie. He was a great boss, but he didn't put up with nonsense. His obvious stress rippled across the deep brown furrows covering his wide forehead.

From Jamie's spot on the ground, six feet beneath those glaring eyes, Mr. Cross looked like the Unjolly Green Giant. Why did this have to happen tonight of all nights? Where had she gone wrong? Jamie had had such big plans to ask her boss for an advance, for extra hours, for at least some of the money she'd need to go to Interlochen. And now, cowering at her boss's feet, Jamie knew she'd be incredibly lucky if she didn't get fired.

chapter.3

I—I," Jamie wished she could talk half as fast as Bren. She tried again, still crouched at the feet of Mark and Mr. Cross. "The smell is from the macaroni fire," she explained. "And then that made me late, you know? So I ran as fast as I could because I really didn't want to be late, especially today. And when I shoved the door open, I didn't know anybody was behind it."

Jamie didn't know if any of it made sense to her boss. How could this be happening to her? To her! Jamie Chandler was the logical one, the dependable one! They could ask anyone who knew her. "Old reliable," Bren called her.

"Jamie," Mr. Cross said, reaching down to help her to her feet, "I'm surprised at you. You know I can't let a place of business turn into a circus. It's the Gnosh Pit—not the mosh pit." He grinned, just a little.

"Excuse me, Mr. Cross," Mark interrupted. Jamie had almost forgotten he was there. "This was all my fault. She didn't do anything wrong." He said it calmly, not sounding at all like a high school kid. His nose had stopped bleeding, although telltale signs were entirely too visible. "I'm fine. OK?" Then Mark walked off before Jamie could thank him.

Mr. Cross sighed. "Well then—no problem . . . no serious problem. Jamie, will you please clean up this mess?"

"Oh yeah," Jamie said. "I mean yes, sir." She felt relieved, though somehow sensing this was still not the best time to ask her boss for that advance.

The door swung open. Jamie and Mr. Cross scrambled out of the way.

"What's with you two?" Maya asked, breezing into the room. She gave her father a kiss on the cheek. "Dad, you weren't being hard on Jamie, were you?"

Maya's younger sister trailed in after her. Morgan, shorter and heavier set than her big sister, wore denim overalls, a faded baseball cap, and a black T-shirt that read, "Save the Seals!" Maya had on a sage silk shirt and matching tribal-print pants, her hair twisted artistically with beaded bamboo hair sticks.

"Dad couldn't be hard on anybody, could you, Dad?" Morgan crooned. "Especially not Jamie."

Jamie watched Mr. Cross's whole personality change around his daughters. He went from polar bear to koala bear in two seconds. For an instant she wondered what it would be like to have one—a dad who transformed when you walked into the room. She shoved the thought from her head.

"It's not your dad's fault," Jamie said. "I'm the problem. I gave Mark over there a bloody nose."

Morgan glanced over at the table of boys next to the window. "Mark from art class?" Morgan had ended up in the same class, even though she was a year younger. "Is he OK?"

"This isn't a hospital," said Mr. Cross, trying to sound gruff, but no longer able to pull it off. "At least not yet. Jamie, shouldn't you be taking orders?"

At least she wasn't fired.

Jamie darted to the kitchen, tied on her apron, washed her hands, and grabbed her pad and pencil. The big white apron hid most of the smoke and nose-crash stains on her shirt.

Morgan pitched in and set up the rest of the tables, while Jamie tried to catch up on orders. Rushing faster than after-football-game warp speed, Jamie took counter orders first—three ice creams, all different. While Maya scooped those orders, Jamie waited the far tables—in order of impatience, the older couple first—until only Mark's table was left.

"Hey, Jamie!" Amber called, sliding into the booth next to Mark's table.

Jamie had been so busy she hadn't even noticed Amber come in. "Hi!" she called. "Be with you in a minute."

Even in her sweat suit, Amber had the eye of every guy at Mark's table. With her silky hair and slender build, Amber

Thomas always made Jamie think of Barbie. Not that Amber was fake. She wasn't. With all her swimming muscles, she'd have been Soccer Barbie or Athletic Barbie.

Maya and Morgan plopped down in Amber's booth. Right away Maya started whispering to Amber, and they both burst into laughter. They were all swimmers—all except Jamie. She didn't have time to be on any team. But she loved helping out whenever she could. It meant spending more time with Harry, a.k.a. "Coach."

Harrison Short had been the Edgewood High swim coach for five years, but Jamie had known him for as long as she could remember. When she was in grade school, she used to color pictures for him and give them to Harry at church. Even back then Harry had talked to her about becoming an artist and using her gifts for God.

"Hello! We're starving over here!"

It was Eric Porter, the only sophomore starter on the football team. Jamie hustled over to Eric and Mark's table. She recognized Steve and Taylor from school and wondered if they even knew her name. Maybe for once being anonymous would be an asset.

"Could I take your order?" she asked, studying her little order pad as if it held the answers to the universe.

"I have a request," Taylor said. "Please don't hurt me!"

They all burst out laughing. At least, Jamie assumed all of them did. She didn't look up from her fascinating order pad.

"What would you like?" she asked softly, digging her pencil into the pad so hard she probably ruined a dozen pages.

"Whoa!" Steve exclaimed. "Anything you want us to have!" Out of the corner of her eye, Jamie could see the palms of his hands, raised in mock self-defense.

Bren would have known what to say. She could have put this tableful of jerks in their place with exactly the right put-down. All Jamie could do was take a deep breath and wish for an Indiana earthquake to swallow them up. Or her.

"We'll have pizza, please," Mark said.

Jamie waited. There were only 274 possible combinations of pizza toppings. She'd figured it out once on a slow night. "What would you like on that?"

"Hey, whatever you want us to have!" Eric said, covering his nose. "I kind of like my nose the way it is."

"Pepperoni," Mark said.

Figures, Jamie thought, getting away as fast as she could. There were creative individuals who ordered red onions and anchovies, or green olives and extra cheese, or straight Italian sausage (her personal favorite). And then there were the pepperoni people.

"And Mountain Dew!" Mark called after her.

Jamie wrote down four MD's. Those guys probably did everything alike.

"Jamie!" Bren strolled into the Gnosh, and the effect was electrical. "Hi, guys!" she said, waving to the counter customers. "Isn't it just too gorgeous outside! What a killer view! The trees are already starting to change colors." She was talking to the whole room. The whole room was listening.

Bren put her hand on Jamie's shoulder just as Jamie was passing in the pizza order. "Take a break, Jamie. We need to talk."

"Everything OK at my house?" Jamie asked, imagining a real fire there.

"Fine!" Bren said. "One of the firemen came back with this water-sucker and vacuumed all the water out of the kitchen. Your mom's shampooing the carpet in the living room."

"Maybe I can break later, Bren," Jamie said, looking around for her boss. Mr. Cross was leaning on Amber's booth, laughing with his daughters about something. "It was pretty rough here earlier, but Mr. Cross looks like he's back in a good mood. Maybe I can still ask for extra hours."

"For the Interlochen deal?" Bren asked.

Jamie nodded.

"That's what I want to talk to you about, girl!" Bren headed for Amber's booth. Bren Mickler had a walk that looked like a skip, it was so bouncy.

"Bren!" Eric called. "Come sit with us!"

"My lap's available!" Taylor called.

Bren smiled sweetly as she passed them. "Sorry, guys. I haven't been interested in adolescent boys since the sixth grade. Enjoy your dinner." Bren hadn't even raised her voice or gotten mad. But she'd as good as poured cold water on the whole group.

Slipping in beside Morgan, Bren started a lively monologue

that had the other girls and Mr. Cross laughing so hard their eyes watered. Jamie heard snatches of the conversation as she delivered orders.

" . . . Jordan . . . macaroni . . . fire trucks . . . giant hose. . . ."

Jamie hoped Mark and the other guys couldn't hear enough of Bren's account to get the whole story. She didn't want Mr. Cross to hear it either. He'd think her whole family was scatter-brained.

"Come over here, Jamie!" Maya called.

Jamie hesitated. She saw Morgan plead with her dad.

"Five-minute break, Jamie," he said. "I'll check orders in the kitchen." He took off.

Jamie pulled up a chair to the end of the booth. She could feel Mark staring at them. Lowering her voice, Jamie said, "Bren, could you keep it down? It's not like I'm dying to have every-body in Edgewood, Indiana, know about the Great Macaroni Fire."

"Never mind that," Amber said. "Jamie, we've been talking about that summer art program in Michigan."

"Interlochen. Did you go to their Web site?" Jamie asked. "Isn't it cool? If I could get into that summer program, I'd have a really good shot at a college scholarship."

"Then you have to go!" Morgan said.

"I'm trying." Jamie glanced over her shoulder and saw Mr. Cross pouring somebody's coffee. "I want to ask your dad for extra hours and maybe an advance. I have to make two thousand fast."

"Two thousand?" Morgan's eyes widened. "Wow!"

"Frankly," Maya said, "I can't see how extra hours around here will get you that kind of money. But if that's what you want . . ." Maya wriggled up to kneeling in the booth and hollered, "Dad! Give Jamie extra hours! OK?"

Jamie was afraid to look around. What if Mr. Cross felt she'd put his daughter up to this?

"Would that be extra hours like tonight's fun?" he called back.

"Dad!" Morgan scolded.

"Oh, alright!" Mr. Cross yelled back. "One minute left on that break, Jamie!"

"Great!" Jamie said. "Thanks, Maya. And Morgan."

"Are you sure this is a good idea, Jamie?" Amber asked. "You've got some pretty tough classes this year. What about your studies?"

Jamie knew Amber didn't mean anything bad, but it needled her just the same. Amber was great at everything. She could get into any college she wanted on a writing scholarship, an athletic scholarship, or even a computer programming grant. And if she didn't, her parents wouldn't have any trouble coming up with tuition.

"If I don't get into a summer art program, Amber," Jamie explained, "all the studying in the world won't do me any good."

"Jamie, you're such a great artist!" Bren insisted. "You should just enter that contest and win your way to Interlochen!"

"Right," Jamie said, pushing back her chair. "I might have

given it a shot if it were any other contest. But a portrait contest? I just don't have anything good enough to send."

"Do a new one," Bren suggested.

"Yeah," Jamie said, getting to her feet. "Just like that. Even if I could sketch something good enough, I'd want to use oils. And I'm just not that good—or fast—with color yet."

"I'll bet you have a portrait that's good enough to send," Bren insisted. "You just don't think it's good enough. You never think anything you do is good enough!"

Jamie put the chair back at the next table, where it belonged. "As much as I'd love to stay and hear the end of my psychological evaluation, duty calls."

"Where's the pizza?" Taylor shouted as Jamie passed their table. She wondered how much they'd overheard. Probably not much. They were too busy trying to flirt with Amber and Bren.

Mark's pizza was up, and Jamie hurried over to their table and set it down on a pile of straw-wrapper spit wads.

"Anything else?" she asked, hoping there wasn't. She tore off their check and set it facedown on the edge of the table.

"Only our pepperoni pizza," Eric snapped.

Jamie felt the breath go out of her. She didn't have to look at the pizza—she could smell the Italian sausage. She flipped over the check. Her own handwriting declared her guilty: It Saus.

"I'll take it back," she muttered. It was her mistake, and it would come out of her paycheck. She reached for the pizza and felt a hand on her wrist.

Jamie looked up and saw Mark. For a second, she stared through his gold wire-rimmed glasses into his deep brown eyes.

"I love Italian sausage," he said quietly.

"But we ordered—" Steve began.

"And it's my turn to buy, right?" Mark said, only now letting go of Jamie's wrist. She could still feel his fingers there.

Jamie didn't see any more of Mark or the others the rest of the evening. They paid Mr. Cross. She wanted to thank Mark, but she couldn't seem to make herself go near their table.

After everybody had gone, Jamie stayed to close and wipe tables. Then Mr. Cross drove her home, and they ironed out her new work schedule.

"Thanks again," she said, hopping out in front of her house.

"Night, Jamie!" He drove home to his wife and daughters. Maya and Morgan had no idea how lucky they were.

As soon as she stepped on the front porch, Jamie remembered the macaroni fire. The house smelled like charcoal—not like a fire, but more like the grill when Bren's dad cooked out for them, or the barbecue pit Coach Short used for the annual swim team picnic.

Maybe Coach Short would have an idea on making money for Interlochen. He had ideas on everything else.

Jessica was already asleep, and Jordan was in their room listening to music. Jamie found Mom sitting up in bed, where she'd fallen asleep over a giant law book. Jamie knew her mom hadn't given up her dream of going back to school and becoming a full-fledged lawyer. With her head back and her mouth slightly open, Jamie's mother looked like a little girl, a tomboy with short, straight hair that framed her suntanned face. People were always mistaking them for sisters, which her mom loved.

Jamie slipped the book out of her hands, noticing how short her mom's nails were. They'd have to have another talk about not biting fingernails. She pulled up the bedspread and turned off the light.

Knowing that there was no way she'd get an ounce of sleep until she checked her computer for smoke damage, Jamie turned it on. She was relieved to hear the familiar loading tones and clicks. She thought about going to TodaysGirls.com, where she knew Bren would be chatting with Amber or Maya.

Instead, Jamie went to Christian Teen Chat and entered the Stranded room. For some reason, this was one cyber room Jamie hadn't passed along to her friends. Maybe it was because she couldn't imagine any of them ever feeling stranded. She'd discovered the chat room over the summer. For over a week Jamie had just eavesdropped on discussions until she got the courage to jump in.

Right away she'd singled out "van_gogh." Some of the teens in Stranded showed up only to cause problems and say things they'd probably never say in person. But van_gogh wasn't afraid to speak his mind.

The first time Jamie actually joined in a chat conversation was to agree with van_gogh, who was arguing that what's inside a person is more important than what that person looks like. When Jamie seconded that idea, someone named Scorpio had typed: "Shut up, fatso."

Van_gogh had clicked her name and invited her into a private, two-way box. They'd chatted for hours about everything. Since then, she had met van_gogh there at least once a week.

Tonight van_gogh wasn't online, but he'd left a message on a bulletin board for her. Excited, Jamie clicked on the message:

rembrandt--do a charcoal portrait. Trust in the talent God's given you, and trust yourself.

chapter.4

J amie almost overslept Tuesday. As soon as she pried her eyes open and her brain kicked in, she remembered van_gogh's message. "Charcoal!" she exclaimed, catapulting herself straight out of bed. A charcoal portrait!

Maybe she'd dreamed the message, imagined van_gogh's bulletin? She should have thought of it herself. Fire, charcoal! The clues were all around her. Maybe she couldn't pull off an oil painting, but a charcoal? She could have used a burned macaroni noodle if they hadn't thrown them all out. She wouldn't have to wait for paint to dry. She actually might be able to pull off a charcoal portrait by the deadline.

Jamie didn't have time to turn on the computer and go look at the message again, but she had no doubt that it was real:

Do a charcoal portrait. Trust in the talent God's given you, and trust yourself.

Who was van_gogh? He knew about the portrait contest and maybe even the fire, with the charcoal idea. It blew her mind to think it was somebody in Indiana, probably in Edgewood. Nothing exotic ever came out of Edgewood, population 28,000, counting the students. Biggest news was word of a new driveway being poured or another elm tree coming down with a disease.

In the back of her mind, Jamie had imagined van_gogh as someone with long hair and haunting eyes on the other side of the world—a sculptor in the outback of Australia, a Dutch painter, a starving French artist. She'd thought of him—yes, she had to admit she believed he was a he—as a college student. Sure, it was a teen chat room. But all you had to do to prove you were a teen was to type in "teen." She knew old weirdos showed up in teen chat from time to time, pretending to be teens.

Amber had warned Jamie and Maya the first time they went online together at her house. "Be careful in chat rooms," she'd said, her tweezed-thin eyebrows knitted together. "Conversation can be fun, but sometimes total wierdos jump up on the screen. You can't tell who the freaks are right away because they use normal names and pretend to be like us.

"So be sure you know someone before you click to a private chat room with them. And never share your personal information. Ever."

Amber might be too perfect, but she knew the Internet better than any of their friends. She told them about the rude Internet users, the profane ones, and the screamers who typed in all capital letters and repeated themselves.

Jamie tested Amber's theories on her own and proved them true. She learned early to simply ignore the freaks. Sometimes their user names would give them away as weirdos, so she just clicked *ignore*, and then none of their ravings appeared on her screen.

She never, ever used her real name or gave out her personal stuff like address, phone number, e-mail account, or even what town she lived in. Amber said there were invisible ways for creeps to trace your location and track you down. And judging from the headlines, this was a real danger to careless people.

So who was van_gogh? The kinds of things he said, he definitely wasn't weird. Maybe he was older. He seemed so wise. Jamie had confided things to van_gogh that she'd never told anybody, not even Bren—dreams and fears, stuff she would have been too embarrassed to talk about face to face.

She could only think of one person she knew who reminded her of van_gogh: Coach Harrison Short. Coach was great to talk to, too. Maybe van_gogh was really Coach. Maybe he just waited for Jamie in the teen chat room. Maybe he only showed up to watch over her, to keep an eye on her like Maya and Morgan's dad kept his eye on them.

"Jamie!" her mother yelled down the hall.

Jamie pulled on her Levi straight-legged jeans and a white jersey top, ran the brush through her hair, and stuck her White Sox baseball cap on backward. She was going to miss most of the swim practice. Even though she just helped out with the team, Jamie usually made it to every practice and every meet.

In two seconds she'd finished washing up and grabbed a breakfast bar from the jelly cupboard.

Jessica, all dressed and clutching her schoolbooks and lunch bag, waited at the table. "Hurry, Jamie!" she pleaded. "I don't want to be late." Jessica never wanted to be late.

"I'll drop you both off," Mom offered, checking her brief-case. "Jordan already left."

Jordan wouldn't be caught dead in her mother's car.

"Thanks, Mom," Jamie said, gulping down a glass of Tang.

They piled into Mom's resurrected Toyota. It sounded like a tank as the engine caught. "You look pretty perky this morning, Jamie," Mom said, backing out of the drive.

"Ah, perky," Jamie teased. "Exactly the look I was going for."

"Mom!" Jessica whined. "I'm going to be late."

"Jessica, you are not going to be late!" Mom promised. "Trust me. We'll drop you off first."

Jess didn't look relieved.

"Are you sure nothing's up, Jamie? Your smile won't shut off this morning. Seriously," Mom pleaded, "if you've got good news, share it! I could use some good news about now. Any good news."

Jamie didn't know how much she should tell her mom. "I

guess I am kind of excited. I'm going to ask Mrs. Woolsey if we can do charcoal portraits in art class."

From the backseat, Jessica made little anxious noises and kicked the back of Jamie's seat.

"Portraits? That will be nice," Mom said. "For the art show? When is it again?"

"A week from Saturday," Jamie answered. It was weird how Jamie kept forgetting about the Edgewood art show. If it hadn't been for the Interlochen summer art program, Jamie's mind would have been filled with the show—even though Emily Eaton would win. Emily always won. If anyone had any doubts, all they had to do was ask Emily.

They dropped Jessica off at Edgewood Elementary, then swung by the high school. Jamie was out before the car had come to a complete stop.

"Wait a minute!" Mom leaned out the window, and Jamie came back. "I'll be home early today. Maybe I'll cook up a real supper."

"Great!" Jamie said, stepping away backward. "I'm pretty sick of pizza. I do have to work an extra hour tonight." She turned and trotted up the walk before her mom could shout objections.

Jamie knew Bren and Amber and everybody would be at the pool for practice. Coach Short would be there, too. Jamie only had ten minutes before first bell. But maybe that would be long enough to find out if van_gogh was really a middle-aged, baby-faced swimming coach who hated to swim.

Echoes streamed from the pool as Jamie opened the door.

The auditorium had the feel of a basement and the smell of old, wet laundry. She looked up at the reverberating *twang* of the diving board and saw Amber make a perfect dive.

"Come on, Coach! The water's fine!" Bren yelled. She knew better. They all knew Harrison Short didn't swim. But all the girls said he was a terrific coach. If Jamie had time, she would have tried out for the team, too.

"Enough fun!" Coach yelled. "To your lanes! Two hundred more yards!"

Maya took off like a submarine leading the rest. Morgan wasn't even in the water. She waved to Jamie, then eased in and started swimming.

"Hi, Jamie!" Coach said as Jamie walked up beside him. He smiled, but studied his stopwatch and kept one eye on the swimmers. "You're late. How's it going? I heard about the fire." He whistled through his teeth, "Yankee Doodle Dandy," the part in the song where he sticks a feather in his cap and calls it macaroni.

"Bren has a big mouth," Jamie muttered. But she was thinking that just like van_gogh, Coach did know about the fire.

"Everybody OK? Your mom get things cleaned up alright?"

"You're welcome to come over and check out the charcoal damage, though." Jamie tried to read his face for a reaction.

"Alright, pull!" he yelled. Quietly, still without taking his gaze off his watch, he said to Jamie, "So, I hear you want to go to Interlochen art school this summer."

He *does* know about the summer program. He *has* to be

van_gogh. "Uh, huh," she said. "I'm trying to earn the tuition. Mr. Cross is letting me work extra at the Gnosh Pit."

"Amber says there's some kind of a contest you can enter?"

He's messing with me, Jamie thought. "I'm thinking about it," she said. If he said anything about a charcoal portrait, she'd have him.

Coach blew the whistle, and the girls hopped out and headed to the locker room. "See you later, Jamie," he said, crossing to his office.

Jamie struggled with her locker so long that she was almost late to art class. The art room stayed so rowdy that Mrs. Woolsey probably wouldn't have noticed her absence anyway. Most of the kids were still floating from table to table, punctuating the room with bursts of laughter. It sounded like elementary school recess.

Jamie slid into her seat, a table she shared with Reese, a sophomore who almost never showed up. She couldn't help sneaking a peek at the last table behind her, Mark's table. He was sitting there, writing something. Jamie wheeled back around before he caught her staring.

"Class! Class!" Mrs. Woolsey's voice always sounded scratchy, like she just woke up. "Take your seats, class!"

Mrs. Woolsey was OK, but Jamie thought she would have made a better kindergarten art teacher. She was batting zero against the high school boys who only took her class because it was an easy B. She loved projects, as opposed to what Jamie considered real art. She combed her gray hair in a pageboy and wore clothes Bren called "retro" and Jamie's mom called "hippie."

"Class," said Mrs. Woolsey, "I owe you an apology today."

"No you don't," said Emily Eaton from her teacher's pet seat, front row center.

Mrs. Woolsey bestowed her best smile on Emily. "Thank you, dear. But I do. Today I was going to introduce Styrofoam animals as an assignment."

"Oooooh," groaned several of the wildest boys.

"But our shipment of Styrofoam didn't get delivered," she continued.

The same chorus of boys cheered. Jamie could hear Bren's cheer, too.

"Which leaves us now in a bad way."

Jamie raised her hand.

"Jamie?" Mrs. Woolsey sounded surprised. Emily and several other girls turned to look.

Jamie never raised her hand in class, even when she knew the answer, which she did a lot of the time. "Um, Mrs. Woolsey, I have an idea."

"Excuse me?" she asked, cupping her hand around her ear, making her long, dream-catcher earrings jiggle.

Jamie said it again over the cackle of the boys behind her. "What if we did portraits? Charcoal portraits?"

Mrs. Woolsey's nose wrinkled, as if Jamie had just asked if the class could mold greasy hairballs or paint each other's toes.

"That's boring," Emily said. "We did that in seventh grade."

But Mrs. Woolsey still hadn't ruled.

"Yes!" Bren shouted. "Portraits! Portraits! Portraits!" She was probably standing in her seat, but Jamie didn't turn to look.

"I just thought portraits might be good for the art show," Jamie said. "And we have everything we need already. Plenty of that thick portrait paper left in our sketchbooks. And I know we've got charcoal pencils in the cabinet."

It may have been Jamie's imagination, but she felt the whole room go fade away. "Fine idea!" Mrs. Woolsey declared at last.

Yes! Way to go, van_gogh! Jamie's mind raced ahead. Now she could use class time and supplies to work on her portrait for the contest! And she could still work extra hours at the Gnosh. Even if she won the contest, she'd still need money for supplies.

"Great idea, Jamie!" Bren cheered from the back.

"Charcoal portraits, class," Mrs. Woolsey repeated. "Emily, will you please pass out the pencils? Morgan and Jamie, pass out the big sketchbooks. Boys, let's get those easels out."

Morgan and Jamie met at the supply closet. Emily pushed between them to get to the cabinet. "Thanks a heap, Chandler!" she muttered.

Morgan's grin covered her whole face. "This is so great, Jamie! Now you can have a portrait for the Interlochen contest!"

Emily slammed the pencil drawer shut and spun around to face them. "Interlochen? As in Michigan? What contest?"

"Oops." Morgan's grin melted, and her eyes begged forgiveness from Jamie.

"Did someone say Interlochen?" Mrs. Woolsey said as she joined them. "What a wonderful school! I had a beau who went to Interlochen. He owns a gallery in New York City now. Are you thinking of going to Interlochen, Emily? That's a grand idea!"

"Do you know anything about a contest to go there?" Emily asked.

"Yes I do!" declared Mrs. Woolsey. "Interlochen has one of the best summer programs for young artists in the nation! Every year they run a contest for . . ."

Jamie watched helplessly as Mrs. Woolsey filled in her favorite student on the contest specifics. "Terrific," Jamie muttered.

"I'm so sorry," Morgan said. "But you can beat her, Jamie! You're tons better than she is! I know you can win."

Jamie shook her head. "Emily would find out sooner or later, I guess." She grabbed a stack of the sketchbooks and turned to pass them out, but her shoulder rammed into somebody. The books toppled from her arms and scattered to the floor.

Mark Wellington, arms protecting his head, hunched in front of her. His charcoal pencil rolled to the floor. Jamie bent down to get it for him, and they bonked heads.

"I-I'm sorry," she stammered.

"I got it," he said, picking up the charcoal pencil, then rubbing the top of his head.

Jamie passed the sketchbooks, slid into her seat, and became invisible. She had to strain to hear what their teacher was saying.

A couple of the guys had started a keep-away game with Bren's charcoal pencil. Bren was obviously enjoying it. Her laughter was the loudest. She'd only signed up for art because Jamie was taking it. Mrs. Woolsey had separated them the first day of class.

Mrs. Woolsey droned on. "Our art show, as you know, will be Saturday morning, a week from this Saturday. We'll have three professional artists as judges, and the newspaper has promised to send a reporter over. I hope you've all told your parents to come. This year the winner of the art show—"

Emily cleared her throat, as if she expected to hear her name announced already, even though nobody had officially entered the show yet.

"—will get $100 in free supplies at Raymond's Art and Hobby Shop."

That would rock! Jamie almost said out loud. She'd need supplies for Interlochen. But she wasn't going to kid herself—not this year. Emily Eaton had won every art show since fourth grade. Why should this be any different? Still, if Jamie could finish her portrait in time for the contest deadline, she'd die happy.

Devon waved his arms at Mrs. Woolsey. "Mrs. Wooly!" he shouted, mispronouncing her name as usual. "I'd like to volunteer my incredible body as our class model. No—don't thank me." He started unbuttoning his shirt.

"Yuck!" "Gross!" Some kids made barfing sounds. Others booed and hissed.

"One more button and I'm outta here!" Bren warned.

"That won't be necessary," said Mrs. Woolsey.

Jamie didn't like wasting all this time. She didn't care who the model was. A portrait is a portrait. She just hoped the model would be somebody interesting, somebody whose soul shined from inside with a depth she could capture in charcoal.

"I think," said their teacher, "that the best thing we can do is form portrait partners."

"Cool! I want Bren!" some guy shouted. Kids yelled out each other's names. Jamie looked around at Bren and Morgan, hoping she would get one of them for her partner.

"Quiet, class!" said Mrs. Woolsey. "I will assign partners." She opened her desk drawer and took out her grade book. "alright, Devon," she said. "I'd like you to partner with Greg." Two by two, she called out pairs of names, like Noah lining up the animals for the ark.

Jamie bit her lip harder as, one after the other, possible portrait partners were eliminated. Morgan got Kristin. Jamie glanced around the room. Mark hadn't been named yet. How embarrassing would it be to have Mark! Bren was left. Jamie hoped she got Bren.

"Bren and . . . Mark," Mrs. Woolsey said, studying her grade book. "And let's see . . . Emily and . . . Jamie!"

Just great! Jamie thought as she jerked her easel into place. *My one shot at a charcoal portrait, and it has to be of Emily Eaton.*

chapter.5

Instantly, Emily was on her feet and at Mrs. Woolsey's desk. They whispered together, Emily gesturing with her hands and Mrs. Woolsey shaking her head from side to side. Finally, with a deep sigh and an even deeper frown, Emily pivoted away from the desk and stomped back to Jamie's table.

"Well, Jamie," Emily said, plunking down her charcoal pencil, "let's get started! I can't wait all day on this. I have a contest to enter."

Mrs. Woolsey had made the school buy enough easels for every student in her advanced art class. This was the first time she'd let Jamie's class use them. Partners had to set the metal stands up back to back. That way each artist could see his or her partner, but not the partner's work-in-progress.

Red-headed Emily Eaton was definitely the cheerleader type,

which worked for her since she was a cheerleader. Her figure was perfect, and her face had nice features, but the smile always looked fake to Jamie.

"We'll need all of our class time to finish our portraits," Mrs. Woolsey reminded them. "But we still have a lot of setting up to do for the art show. Would anyone like to volunteer to help me in the afternoons after school?"

Jamie would have helped if she could have. But she had her hands full with the extra hours at the Gnosh.

"I'll help, Mrs. Woolsey!" Emily said.

"I'll help, Mrs. Woolsey," Bren mimicked from the cheap seats in the back of the room.

"Thank you, Emily," said Mrs. Woolsey, bestowing a warm smile on her pet. "I can always count on you, dear."

"So you can be sure to get the best booth for your art?" Jamie whispered to Emily.

Emily shot her a sly grin. "Why not? If you're so worried about a good spot, why don't you help?"

Jamie was pretty sure Emily knew she worked after school. She wasn't going to give the girl the satisfaction of hearing her complain about it. Instead she gritted her teeth. "Let's draw."

Angry black lines took form on Jamie's paper, much too dark. She had to get hold of her anger. That's not what she wanted to show in her portrait for the contest. She wanted something deep. But the only thing deep about Emily Eaton was her dad's wallet.

"Will you hold still?" snapped Emily. "How am I supposed to capture your portrait if you keep bobbing around like that? And stop frowning! This is important, you know."

Jamie crossed her eyes at Emily. On Jamie's paper, Emily's chin line grew longer and longer. She felt like adding a goatee and a mustache. But she knew she had the proportions right. And the shape—that was right, too.

Mrs. Woolsey floated around the room. From time to time, Jamie caught snippets of her critiques. "Devon, turn the paper right side up!" "Morgan, try to use more of the total surface area." "Mark, that's an interesting angle. I like it. Keep going." "Bren, Bren, Bren," she scolded.

Mark was pretty good. Jamie knew that. He'd come up with the best copper etching. Mark had etched an entire scene, while the rest of them had settled for a single object. She just hoped Bren wouldn't blab to him about the Interlochen contest. That's all she needed—more competition.

"That is not funny, Andrew!" Mrs. Woolsey scolded. "Michael does not have long, pointy ears like that!"

Finally, Mrs. Woolsey worked her way over to Jamie. Jamie felt her teacher's breath on her neck as she peered over her shoulder. She said something that sounded like "crumb," but might have been "hmmmm."

Mrs. Woolsey moved around to Emily's work. "Oh, very nice, Emily!" she exclaimed. "Now, don't you think you have her cheeks too wide here?" She rubbed on the paper, then took the pencil out of Emily's hand. "And Jamie's eyes are more this shape." She scratched and blended, narrowed her eyes at Jamie, and drew some more. "See? Hairline dips like that."

Since the first week of class, Mrs. Woolsey had probably done as much on Emily's artwork as Emily had. She'd tried to put her hands on Jamie's paper the first day of class, and Jamie had freaked. Mrs. Woolsey hadn't tried again.

But Emily liked the help. She'd always gotten their art teachers to "help." Jamie had a feeling Mrs. Woolsey had no idea how much of her own effort went into Emily's art. No wonder the teacher always liked Emily's work, Jamie thought. It was mostly hers anyway.

Mrs. Woolsey was really going at Emily's paper now. "See the mouth take shape when you shade it like this? There!" She gave back Emily's pencil. "Nice job, Emily. Really coming along nicely."

Jamie shut out everything else and worked. She had all Emily's features in exactly the right places. It was even starting to look like her. But it was no good. The portrait had no heart, no soul. How on earth could she ever stand out in a pile of portraits with this? She set down her charcoal pencil. It was no use.

"If I win that portrait contest with this picture of you, it will be a miracle!" Emily exclaimed.

Jamie stared up at her. "What?" Jamie didn't think she'd heard her right. Was this a new Emily? The old Emily never would have said that. What Jamie lacked in confidence, she could have gone and bought from the excess at the Emily Confidence Storehouse. "Did you say it would be a miracle if you won the contest?"

"Yes!" Emily sighed and shook her head. "And it will be all your fault. How can I draw your pug nose? If I get it right, nobody will believe it's real."

That did it. Jamie took her charcoal and started reworking Emily's mouth. She didn't even realize Mrs. Woolsey was behind her until her teacher cleared her throat.

"Jamie, no, no, no!" she chided. "You've got it all wrong! Emily's mouth is not nearly as big as that."

The buzzer sounded for second period. Jamie tore off her paper and wadded it up. "You wanna bet?"

Jamie, Bren, and Morgan walked down the hall together, fending off the sea of students herding in both directions. At least a dozen kids said "Hi" to Bren.

"How's your portrait coming, Jamie?" Morgan asked.

"It's not," Jamie answered.

"Mark's really nice," Bren said. "I'm no good at portraits, but he sure is. Gotta go! Later."

What would van_gogh say now? Jamie wondered as she sat through her morning classes. She'd wasted her first day of portrait drawing. How would she ever pull off a contest-winning portrait of Emily Eaton?

In study hall, Jamie remembered she'd forgotten to read the story for English, but she skimmed it before class. That wasn't like her. She'd rather study all night than show up without her homework done.

Her day didn't get any better. At lunch the cafeteria served, of all things, pizza—pepperoni, of course—as if she needed a reminder of Mark and his friends and the Gnosh disaster, as if she didn't already have entirely too much pizza in her life. She tripped going up the stairs to sixth period and bruised her shin, not to mention crumpling her math paper.

By the end of the day, Jamie was so tired she couldn't see how she'd get her homework done and put in the extra hour at the Gnosh Pit. But she had to. She'd have a better chance of earning the two thousand than she would winning a portrait contest with Emily Eaton's big mouth.

After school, Jamie hurried to Coach Short's office. She wished she had hours to hang out with him. He took one look at her and asked, "What's the trouble, Jamie? You look like you've lost your best paintbrush."

"Something like that." Jamie plopped into the big wooden chair across from Coach. He leaned back and put his feet up on his desk. "I don't know what to do, Coach," she said. "I really want to go to the Interlochen art camp this summer. I was going to try to do a portrait for the contest, but that's not working."

"Come on now, Jamie," Coach said. "God's given you a talent. Use it!"

It was almost what van_gogh had written.

"I want to!" Jamie said, louder than she'd meant to. "But I think I have a better shot at earning the money than winning the contest."

"Have you talked to your mother about it?" Coach pulled his legs off the desk and leaned forward, his hands clasped in front of him.

"What do you mean?" Jamie asked.

"I mean that woman who gave birth to you—your mother." Jamie grinned. "No. Not exactly."

"What I mean," Coach said, locking his gaze on her so she couldn't look away, "is that your mother would want to help you with the tuition if there's any way she can."

"We're having trouble making our rent," Jamie said. *And keeping our car running, and paying the electric bill,* she thought.

"I know," he said, making Jamie wonder how much he did know. She wondered if he had known her father before he took off. "Maybe your mom has something put away for a rainy day," he went on. "You look like you're in the middle of a downpour. I'm just saying, don't you think it's worth at least talking to her about this?"

"Maybe you're right," Jamie said, feeling a surge of hope and possibility again. "Mom wants me to be an artist—as long as I'm not a starving artist. It won't hurt to ask her. I could pay her back when I get the money. Thanks, Coach!"

Jamie practiced her speech in her head as she walked home. She'd open with a plug about a good college. Mom must have told them a thousand times that she wanted them to go to college. Jamie would explain about portfolios and all the great pieces of art she could complete at the summer camp. Then she'd ease into Interlochen and tell her what Mrs. Woolsey said about its great art program. Last, she could describe the summer art camp. And when she had Mom right where she wanted her, she'd ask for the money.

It felt great to be in the crisp air of early autumn. Bright sunshine spotlighted the few yellow leaves on still-green trees and the burnt umber shadows in tree branches. She loved the spongy feel of the grass and the clean, minty smell of pines as she turned onto her own street.

Jamie hopped up the steps to her front porch and stopped. For a second she wondered if she were in the wrong place. Angry voices poured out of this house. Jamie's mother almost never yelled.

But her mother *was* yelling. "How could you? How could you?"

Jamie tiptoed in, although they wouldn't have heard her if she'd ridden in on elephants. She stood in the doorway of the kitchen and stared dumbly at Jordan and Jessica sitting at the kitchen table while their mother waved a piece of paper in Jordan's face.

Mom's back was to Jamie. "Two hundred dollars in phone bills, Jordan! Do you have any idea how much that is?" Jamie couldn't remember ever seeing her mom this angry.

"About two hundred dollars?" Jordan muttered.

"This is not funny, young lady!" Mom screamed. "You have been calling that boy behind my back!"

"You like Mike," Jordan said.

"I liked Mike when he lived here!" Mom shouted. "I don't like Mike three hundred miles away! Not long-distance!"

"It's not fair!" Jordan shouted back. "He's still my best friend! He's my boyfriend! That doesn't change just because he moved away!"

"We had a deal," Mom said in a controlled, forced voice that Jamie considered worse than the shouting voice. "One ten-minute call a week."

"One? Everybody else gets to call their boyfriends every single night!"

"Everybody else? Jordan, you know better than that! How could you—"

"She's really sorry," Jessica said softly, cringing as if they had one of those mothers who hit kids.

"Stay out of it, Jess," Mom said.

Jessica slumped in her chair as if all of her bones had evaporated.

Jordan finally noticed Jamie. "What about her? Jamie gets to have a job and earn money for stuff. It's not fair! You won't even give me money for the Halloween dance!"

"That's not true, Jordan," Mom said. "I said you could go."

"Without a costume? With a dumb sheet again? Sixty-five dollars. That's all I need for the Cinderella gown. And Mike said he could come back and be Prince Charming and go with me."

Mom closed her eyes and stared up at the ceiling, making a growling noise Jamie had never heard before.

Jessica joined in with squeaky little whimpers.

Mom looked at Jess, and Jamie could see her soften. "It's alright, Jessica," she said. "Jordan and I are just having a discussion. And honey, don't worry about your school. Of course we'll pay the book fee. They won't make you turn in your books just because I haven't sent them a check yet. I told you. I'll write a note and explain and ask for a week's extension. It's nothing serious, honey."

Poor Jessica looked like she thought they'd throw her in prison.

Mom sighed, ran her fingers through her thin blonde hair, and looked at Jamie. "Why are you lurking in the doorway?" She shook her head and said more softly, "I'm sorry, Jamie. Is something wrong?"

"No, no. Everything's fine." How could she ask for money in the middle of all this?

"Something is wrong," Mom insisted. "I can see it all over your face. What is it? You might as well come out with it now."

On the one hand, Jamie reasoned, chewing the inside of her cheek, could there be a worse time than right now to hit up Mom for cash? But on the other hand, if Jamie didn't get her request in soon, Jordan would keep needling Mom until she caved and blew money on the stupid Halloween dress.

"Jamie?" Her mother's voice sounded strained, with anger creeping back into it.

"I need two thousand dollars to go to art camp this summer." Jamie spit it out in one breath. It wasn't at all like she'd planned.

Mom looked as if she'd just been delivered the final blow that would send her toppling backwards. A silence fell over the kitchen. Nobody moved. Nobody spoke.

Jessica was the one to break the silence. "Jamie should go to the art camp. And Jordan should go to the Halloween party. And I want to pay for my books on time." Jessica's forehead folded into tiny wrinkles a nine-year-old should never have. She stood up, and her chair squeaked on the linoleum. She walked over to Mom and gave her a hug. "It will be OK," she said. "I'm going to ask Daddy for the money."

chapter.6

Jessica walked out of the kitchen, but her words stayed: "I'm going to ask Daddy for the money." Jessica had never even met her dad, never spoken to him, never gotten a letter from him. She wasn't even born until four months after he left them.

"She wouldn't recognize her daddy if he walked up and did somersaults around her," Jamie said. "Which is about as likely as having him suddenly turn up and give us money." Jamie felt bad as soon as she'd said it, but it was true.

"You don't know!" Jordan argued. "Maybe he would give me sixty-five dollars if I asked him, if I told him what it was for."

"Oh yeah?" Jamie said. Jordan didn't know their daddy any better than Jessica did. "Let's see. How old were you the last time you heard from him? Were you three yet, Jordan? Ask him for the money? You might as well ask the tooth fairy!"

"Stop it, girls!"

Jamie looked at her mother. Her eyes were red. She swiped at her tears with the back of her hand.

Jamie felt like crying, too. She ran out of the kitchen and down the hall to her room. *Don't cry,* she commanded herself. *Don't cry.* She felt the sadness harden, solidify into a ball of anger that sank into her soul. *Don't let him make you cry again!*

She tried not to think about how hard she'd cried when her dad walked out without one word to her, with nothing but the slam of the door.

Jamie knew she should talk to God, tell God how she felt and try to turn her anger over to him. That's probably what her mother did. But it was so hard—like a deep wound that could be scraped open at any moment, letting out a flow of rage. Why did everything have to be so hard? Even the good things! Her talent, for example. Why was it so hard to do what van_gogh had said and trust her own talent?

Suddenly, Jamie wanted nothing more than to talk with van_gogh. She turned on the computer and clicked straight through to the Christian Teen Chat home page. A message appeared in a small, gray box labeled Friends:

van_gogh is online.

She clicked on his name and was sent to the Stranded room. At the top of the screen came the words: "Welcome, rembrandt. You are in Christian Teen Stranded room."

Searching for van_gogh, she saw a long discussion in progress about which date it was OK to have a first kiss on.

Why don't they just take it to the Dating and Relating room? Jamie wondered. She typed in her dialog box:

rembrandt: van_gogh, r u here?

Immediately, a box sprang to life in the corner of her screen, and van_gogh's message appeared in green letters:

van_gogh: kewl! waiting 4 u.

Jamie added the minutes in her mind. If van_gogh was really Coach, could he have had enough time to get home, hang out with his boys, and then get online? Probably. Jamie didn't even care anymore. She had to talk to van_gogh, no matter who he was.

van_gogh: u still there rembrandt?

Jamie started typing and couldn't stop. She typed in her whole day—the portrait, Emily, pepperoni pizza, the free-for-all with her mom and sisters. She even told him all she could remember about her father and how he'd left them stranded.

> rembrandt: sometimes i wonder if he still has long black hair like Jessica. i hate it when my little sis is sad. : (
>
> van_gogh: i feel like that about my little brother. i'd do anything for him.
>
> rembrandt: when i try to picture my dad, he always has a paintbrush in his hand. mom says he was a good artist fwiw. if he was and if he made $, he didn't leave us any.
>
> van_gogh: maybe he did.
>
> rembrandt: trust me. he didn't!! :-[
>
> van_gogh: i mean, maybe he left things behind, even shoes or clothes or books. IMHO, those things belong to you. You could sell them and use the $ for art camp.

Dad had left stuff behind. Jamie knew it. She hadn't thought about it for years, but she remembered seeing Mom carrying all kinds of junk to a corner of the attic and then warning Jamie to stay out of it. Mom had been crying. Much later, Jamie had sneaked to the attic and uncovered old high school albums, prom napkins, and photographs of them as a family. She'd stared at the family pictures, each smile digging a hole inside of her, deeper and deeper. She hadn't gone back since.

rembrandt: van_gogh, u r a genius! PBT! Thanx! BFN

Jamie started to click on *exit,* when she saw another message line come up:

van_gogh: remember--trust yourself and the talent God gave you.

Jamie tiptoed down the hall and out to the garage. The attic was more like a crawlspace in the ceiling. Taking a broom handle, she poked at the white square of plaster that led to the attic. It moved, and she pushed it to one side.

Dad, she thought as she pulled a crate under the opening and climbed up, *you are going to pay for my art camp whether you like it or not.* She pulled herself through the hole, but it was too dark to see anything. She jumped down, got a flashlight, and climbed back up.

Splaying the beam of light around the narrow attic, Jamie had second thoughts. Everything smelled like wet cardboard. In the corner she spotted mouse droppings, but didn't see any mice. Cobwebs streaked across the rafters. The near side of the attic held boxes and boxes of papers and notebooks—probably Mom's taxes and records and school stuff.

She shined the light on the far corner, where she knew Mom had put Dad's stuff at least eight years ago. At first after Dad left, Mom had said over and over that he would be back. By the time she dumped his things in the attic, Mom had stopped talking about Dad, and Jamie had stopped asking.

Crouching and shivering, she made her way to the pile. The scrapbooks and journals were in the first box she came to. Jamie didn't even give them a second look. The next box was filled with notebooks, and the margins had little sketches and doodles all over them.

"Junk!" she muttered. There had to be something worth selling. People were always wanting other people's old things. They called them antiques. She pulled out a gold sweater with EPH on the back, a high school letter sweater, riddled with holes. There was a lava lamp—broken; a clock—no hands; a pair of boots—both for the left foot, and half a dozen ashtrays from the Holiday Inn.

"Just great," Jamie muttered. This wasn't going to be any help at all. An old moth-eaten blanket was thrown over something. Probably another stupid box of stupid junk. Frustrated, Jamie whipped off the blanket. There, under the old blanket, was a big, beautiful art portfolio. She wiped the dust off the top. It was real leather, a yard wide, the kind professional artists used to carry their paintings. She inhaled and could smell something like cooked cherries under the must.

She lifted the case out of the rubble. The leather was well worn, but the portfolio was in perfect condition. Even better, it was already broken in. Nobody had one like this, not even Mrs. Woolsey.

Jamie knew she could probably sell the portfolio for a hundred dollars. But there was no way she'd ever sell this. This was going to be her inspiration. Jamie would fill this portfolio with artwork that would have those college recruiters begging her to come to their schools! Next year she'd be going to art evaluation days, standing in lines with other hopeful artists, waiting to see college recruiters who would review her portfolio and decide if she deserved a scholarship. Nobody would look more worthy than she did.

"Jamie! Where are you? Shouldn't you be going to work?" Mom was calling from inside the house.

Jamie grabbed the portfolio and scurried down. She looked both ways before racing through the house to her room, where she shoved her prize under the bed. She could hardly wait to clean it up and start her new life as a professional artist.

Compared to the night before, Tuesday at the Gnosh Pit turned out to be slow and uneventful. Jamie found herself looking for Mark, but he'd probably never come back—not while she was working anyway. Not even Maya or Morgan stopped by. They were probably chatting in the private TodaysGirls.com chat room.

Mr. Cross made her go home early. He still didn't like her working late on school nights. Neither did Mom.

Mom was sitting at the kitchen table, papers spread out in front of her, when Jamie walked in.

"Hi, Mom," Jamie said cautiously, testing the waters.

Mom took off her reading glasses and sent Jamie a crooked smile. "Sorry about all the craziness this afternoon, Jamie."

"Me too," she said.

"You know I'd do anything for you, honey. I'm just not sure we can swing the art camp this summer. Maybe next summer—"

"It's OK, Mom," Jamie said. It wasn't OK, but Jamie couldn't stand to see her mom hurting. It wasn't Mom's fault they didn't have money. "How's Jess?"

Mom sighed and shook her head. "She'd probably love a visit from her big sis."

Jamie knocked on her sisters' room. She could hear Jordan's rap music, even though her sister always wore headphones. *One day,* she thought, adding one more worry to the pile, *Jordan's going to break her eardrums.*

She thought she heard Jessica's little voice say, "Come in." Jamie closed the door behind her and crossed the room to Jessica's bed. Jordan was doing homework at her desk, bobbing and weaving to her CD. They exchanged waves.

Sitting on the edge of Jessica's bed, Jamie watched her little sister frown over the letter she was writing. Jessica sat very straight, propped by pillows against the headboard.

"How do you spell *grateful*?" Jessica asked, not looking up from her pencil and paper. Her damp, black hair spread over her pink flannel nightgown, and she smelled like baby powder.

Jamie spelled *grateful* for her. "You alright?" she asked, wishing she knew what else to say.

"Umm-hmm," Jessica answered. "I'm almost finished."

Jamie could have pointed out that nobody knew where to mail the letter. They might as well address it to the North Pole. Instead she said, "You're a good writer, Jessica. Maybe you should write books when you grow up."

Jessica smiled up at her. "And I'll hire you to draw all my pictures." Jess threw her arms around Jamie's neck. "I love you, Jamie."

Jamie had to swallow hard. "I love you, too, Jess."

After getting ready for bed and finishing her history report, Jamie still had time to check into TodaysGirls.com. She missed her friends, missed watching swim practice, missed the time she usually got to spend chatting with them online.

The "room" was full.

faithful1: we've missed you, rembrandt!

nycbutterfly: how was it @ the Gnosh????? busy? Dad behave himself?

rembrandt: me 2. not busy. yep. tough to get a word in edgewise with you chatters. reminds me—where's chicChick, Queen of Chat?

chicChick: i hear that, rembrandt! LOL! true, i have been chatting a lot tonite. r your ears burning? :*)

rembrandt: ?????????

nycbutterfly: jellybean says u hate your portrait of emily + the contest deadline is a week from tomorrow! can u pull it off by then?

rembrandt: can't see how. & NW i can get $ from Mom. hopeless, I know.

faithful1: rembrandt, r u totally sure u don't have something u can send in? think about it! don't be so hard on yourself.

chicChick: RO! i just no u have something great u r sitting on cuz u think it's not good enuf!

rembrandt: trust me. nothing is good enuf for the contest.

Jamie thought about sharing her great find in the attic. But Bren wouldn't rest until she knew where it had come from. And Jamie just didn't feel like getting into anything about her dad tonight. Suddenly, she couldn't wait to pull the portfolio from under her bed and look at it again. She might even have time to clean it up tonight. Then she could just show it to them tomorrow.

Bren was already off on another subject.

chicChick: can anybody tell me how they can clone sheep and take pictures of Mars, but they can't figure out how to get rid of zits?

rembrandt: time for bed. CUL8r

faithful1: me 2. TTYL.

nycbutterfly: CU! BFN!

chicChick: hey! where'd everybody go???? OK TTFN!

Jamie logged off and shut down her computer. In the bathroom under the sink she found what she needed—neat's-foot oil. Hurrying back to her room, she pulled the portfolio out from under her bed.

She stared down at it a moment, tracing its narrow stitches with her fingertip. The case was as amazing as she'd remembered. Starting with the handle, she cleaned and buffed the top, the front, the back, the bottom. With each stroke, the leather warmed to a deep mahogany, and the rich cherry scent mingled with a rugged Western aroma that made her want to close her eyes and inhale.

It would probably be enough just to wipe out the insides. Jamie pressed the gold latch that still worked perfectly and flipped back the cover flap. Something was inside, pressed against the back of the portfolio. She reached in and pulled out a large sheet of art paper.

Even before she wiped the dust off with her sleeve, Jamie knew it was good. Her heart sped up. It was a watercolor, a 14x16. A portrait.

Jamie stared at the young face, the full lips, the tiny turned-up nose, the big brown eyes that stared back at her. There was no doubt at all in her mind. This was the work of her father. And the portrait was of her.

chapter.7

Wednesday morning Jamie got up before the sun. The first thing she did was pull out her portfolio and take out the portrait. She blew off a thin layer of dust. In the bottom right corner was a label: *Jamie's Portrait*.

Propping the drawing against her bed, Jamie stepped back and studied it. It was so weird. Her head was shaped the same, her eyes hadn't changed, and already the nose was pug. Jamie guessed she'd been about five years old when her dad had drawn the portrait. Sparks of memory surfaced—Jamie on a stool, bright light, her dad in constant motion, frowning behind an easel.

The portrait was better than good. Her dad had captured something, a childlike innocence that was so real Jamie wanted to reach into the portrait and pull it back. He hadn't just drawn her outsides, the way she looked—although the features were exactly right. He had captured what had been inside her before he left.

Jamie looked in her mirror. Her features hadn't changed that much, but she didn't see the childlike trust staring back at her, not like she saw from the eyes in *Jamie's Portrait.* What her father had drawn was so amazing, so full of creative genius and talent. She felt she would never do anything half as good.

Jamie shoved the portrait into her portfolio and got ready for school. She found her oldest Levi's, pulled them on, and slipped into her plain green, long-sleeved T-shirt. She brushed her hair, slid on a headband, then changed her mind and pulled off the green headband in favor of the hat she'd won in the seventh-grade art show. It read "Smart Art!" in white letters on faded green, the award to the honorable mentions in the show. Emily had won first place and a trophy.

Grabbing her backpack and portfolio, she made her way down the hall. Mom's alarm went off just as Jamie passed her room. She hollered in, "Morning, Mom! I'm going in early to help Coach. I'll walk. I love you!"

Jamie could feel some of her frustration seep out as she strode across lawns that sparkled with dew, her portfolio swinging beside her. A big orange sun crept up behind an empty lot, sending streaks of pink and purple in all directions. She thought about what van_gogh had said about God-given talent.

"Nobody can paint the sky like you do!" she shouted up. She

glanced around to see if anyone had heard her, but nobody else was on her street. God obviously knew a lot about art. If God had really given her a talent for art, maybe she could pull off this portrait thing.

Jamie took the shortcut, feeling the chilly dew seep through her tennis shoes. The side door to the high school was locked, but the janitor came when she tapped on the glass. "Morning, Mr. Strickland," she said as he held the door open for her.

"Good morning, Ms. Chandler!" Mr. Strickland was the nicest janitor she could imagine. He looked more like a professor or a stockbroker, dressed better than most of the teachers, and he remembered everybody's name, always calling them Mr. or Ms. "You're here ahead of schedule, are you not?"

"Trying to make up for lost time," Jamie explained, juggling her backpack and portfolio. "I've missed helping out at a couple of swim practices."

"I don't think Harry is even here yet."

"That's OK, Mr. Strickland. I'll go ahead and start cleaning up. Thanks."

Jamie walked down the empty halls of Edgewood High School, surprised by the weird echo of her own footsteps. The *squeak, plop* of her wet shoes seemed louder than the hall-crowd noise when hoards of students jockeyed for position between classes.

As she pushed through the glass doors to the pool entrance, she flipped on the light and was greeted by things left undone because she hadn't been there. Benches needed straightening, the storage room needed to be organized. The towels were in the wrong place, and the wall clock looked off by at least five minutes. Leaning her portfolio against the wall in the corner, she dug in.

Jamie was checking the scoreboard when she heard Bren's laugh. Then a tangle of other familiar voices came her way. They burst through the doors.

"Jamie!" Maya cried.

"You beat us here?" asked Amber.

The others greeted her, then ran to the locker room to suit up.

"Thanks for coming in so early, Jamie," Coach said, opening his office door. "Don't know what I'd do without you."

Jamie followed him in, feeling calmer, better than she had in a couple of days. Coach had that effect on her. He always had—just like van_gogh.

He gave her some duties—copying practice times, recording hours, looking up phone numbers. It felt good to be working with Coach. Jamie wondered if this was how daughters felt about their fathers.

"So," Coach was saying, "last weekend the boys wanted to go camping. You know how I love hiking in the fall. So I packed up the wife and kids—actually I made the boys lists."

Harrison Short was very big on lists. Jamie tried not to smile as he described the campout. She could imagine General Short barking orders to his disorderly troops. But she knew he would do anything for them.

"I had a great time, but the boys were miserable. All three

came out with a good case of poison ivy." He lowered his voice. "How are you doing, Jamie? Talk to your mom?"

"Yeah, bad timing. But I'm still trying to come up with a portrait in time for the contest. And I'm picking up extra money at the Gnosh."

A big splash came from the pool, and Jamie and Coach Short went out to watch. Amber started easy warmup laps. Maya and Bren dived in at the same time, with Bren yelling, "Come on in, Coach and Jamie!" Morgan dipped her toe in the pool and moved her foot around.

Amber was a swimming machine, cutting through the clear water straight and steady.

"Amber is such a strong swimmer," Jamie said.

"She's good," Coach admitted. "But Amber also works harder at it than anybody I know. You have to work hard, even when God's given you talent."

Jamie started to ask Coach if he was really talking about her and her art talent. But he blew his whistle before she could. "Practice flip-turns! Don't ease up! Make 'em clean!"

Jamie determined she would work on her art the way Amber worked at her swimming. She could work harder than anybody else on a portrait for the contest, even a portrait of Emily Eaton. From now on, she simply would not allow Emily's big mouth to get in the way.

Practice ended. While the girls changed out of their suits, Jamie retrieved her portfolio.

"Nice bag!" called Coach Short. "Too bad it's not practical. Too flat to carry much of anything, if you ask me."

Jamie pretended to be offended. "Excuse me? This is a professional artist's portfolio, thank you very much."

Coach narrowed his blue eyes and adjusted his glasses. "Looks kind of like a giant leather envelope, doesn't it?"

"Port-fo-li-o," Jamie said, enunciating every syllable in a way that would have made her English teacher proud.

"Sor-r-ry!" Coach said with a laugh. "Artistic temperament."

Jamie strutted down the hall, now teeming with bodies. A couple of kids did double takes of her portfolio. But nobody said anything about it until she walked into art class.

It was probably the earliest she'd ever been to art class, but Emily and Mrs. Woolsey looked as if they'd been in deep conversation for hours. Emily turned from her seat on Mrs. Woolsey's desk. "Where did you get that?"

Jamie tried to lean the portfolio against her desk, but it kept sliding down and blocking the aisle. "Oh this? I've had it for a while."

Mrs. Woolsey came over to investigate. Her skirt swished in time to her clicking heels. "Isn't that lovely!" she exclaimed. "What a wonderful portfolio!" She lifted it and examined it front and back.

"I've never seen you carry that before," Emily said, sounding as if she thought Jamie might be on the FBI's list of Most Wanted Art Thieves.

"Let's set it over here out of the way," said Mrs. Woolsey, moving the portfolio to the wall at the end of Jamie's aisle, next to a metal cabinet.

Jamie would have preferred to keep it close by, but the portfolio, nestled between the wall and the cabinet, stayed in place and was out of the way. So she left it and started setting up her easel.

A couple of sophomores were checking out Jamie's portfolio when Morgan and Bren walked in together. Jamie got up to meet them. "Come look what I found in the attic," she whispered.

Bren dropped to her knees dramatically in front of the portfolio. "I love it!" she shouted.

"It's gorgeous, Jamie," Morgan said.

"This is so cool!" Bren squealed. "Now all you have to do is admit you have great art to go in it, right? Then you take it to colleges and show them your stuff, right?"

"Kind of," Jamie said.

"Class!" Mrs. Woolsey shouted. "Get those easels set up, please! Think of the art show!"

Jamie hurried back to her spot, leaving Morgan and Bren still admiring her new portfolio. She wasn't looking forward to spending the next hour with Emily Eaton, but she was determined to draw a great portrait in spite of the girl.

Before most of the other students had even filtered back to their own places, Emily and Jamie had their easels back to back, artist pads in place, and charcoal pencils aimed at each other, like a Wild West shootout.

"Take the hat off!" Emily whined. "Isn't that the one everybody got in some art fair I won?"

Don't let her get to you, Jamie told herself. *Your art and your talent—that's all that matters. Not Emily.*

"You better keep your face from scrunching so much today," Emily said. "I think you're doing it on purpose so I won't win the Interlochen contest. You're trying to mess up my portrait."

Jamie scrunched her face. She couldn't help herself. "Don't worry, Emily," she said. "Mrs. Woolsey will always fix it for you."

Jamie started over with a fresh piece of paper. She stared at it, trying to visualize the portrait she had only to discover. Real works of art, she believed, already existed, waiting for the artist to bring them to life so others could see them.

But Emily had a whole different look, a stark contrast from the day before. Instead of curly, shoulder-length red hair, a tight knot sat on top of her head. Emily had pulled it so tight her eyes looked slanted. And her makeup was different, too.

It doesn't matter, Jamie told herself as she drew her first lines. She was starting over anyway. The shape of the head appeared on Jamie's paper. Then the curve of the chin, the position of the eyes, and the location of the cheek bones. They all fell into place.

From the back of the room came an outburst of giggles.

Jamie recognized Bren's laugh when she heard it. She glanced back and saw Bren doubled over with laughter, one hand resting on Mark's shoulder.

Focus! Jamie told herself.

"Mrs. Woolsey, tell Mark to stop it!" Bren shouted, punctuating each word with a giggle.

Jamie tried to concentrate, but Bren's cackles interrupted her about every ten seconds. And Mark was laughing, too! The portrait she'd envisioned on that blank paper faded. Everything was wrong, all wrong.

"Quit frowning!" Emily whined. "How am I supposed to get your eyebrows right when you do that?"

"Mrs. Woolsey?" Bren called. "Could I do Mark blindfolded?"

"Good idea!" shouted Andrew. "Markie would look a lot better in a blindfold. How about a whole mask?"

The class erupted in laughter.

"Not that!" Bren protested. "I mean I'd like to blindfold myself and draw Mark's face by touch, the way blind people do. Maybe I could get his nose right that way. I've got his eyes crooked and his mouth falling off his chin—" Bren reached over her easel and put her hand over Mark's face. "Like this! See? Otherwise, I'm just not getting it."

Of course she wasn't getting it, Jamie thought. Bren didn't even like art. She'd be the first one to admit she couldn't draw real people or objects. She couldn't even trace them! The only reason she got by in art class was that she could fake it with Styrofoam and linoleum and paper clips.

"Ooooh, Mark!" somebody said. "You better be careful! She's way out of your league!"

"You're just jealous, Larson!" Andrew yelled back.

How was Jamie expected to work in an environment like this? In a class like this? With a teacher like this? With a subject like this? . . . With a friend like this?

chapter.8

The bell sounded for second block. Jamie wanted to get out of there before Bren and Mark did. She ripped her drawing from its book, folded it in half, and slid it into the wastebasket on her way out.

Jamie heard Bren holler after her, "Jamie! Wait up!"

But she pretended not to hear as she weaved through kids jamming the halls. Why did she feel like this? What did she care what Bren and Mark did in art class?

Alone, she took her seat by the window in chemistry class and tried not to think about Mark and Bren. She stared out at the parking lot crowded with cars and imagined sneaking out the window, jumping in one of those cars, and driving away as far as she could.

Mr. Kistler, her chemistry teacher, had taken roll and passed out a quiz when Jamie suddenly remembered her portfolio. She'd left it in art class.

"Mr. Kistler!" she called, waving her hand.

"No questions, please. Everyone quiet and do your own work," he said, sitting behind his desk and opening his book.

"But Mr. Kistler!" Jamie pleaded. "I left my portfolio in the art room. Can I go get it, please?"

"It will keep," he said.

"But I—"

"Take your quiz," he said, rubbing his mustache the way he always did when he got mad at them. "You're disturbing the class."

Jamie tried to tell herself her portfolio would be fine. Nobody could exactly walk out with it without being noticed. She took the quiz, grateful she'd at least read the chapter and knew most of the answers.

It seemed like the longest chemistry class in the history of time. The second the bell sounded, Jamie was out of her chair and running down the hall to the art room.

"Jamie Chandler, walk in the halls!" yelled the principal.

Jamie power-walked the rest of the way and got there while the room was still spewing out freshmen. There, between the file and the wall, rested her portfolio, right where she'd left it. As Jamie rescued it, she felt relief surge through her.

"You left your portfolio, Jamie!" Mrs. Woolsey called.

Really? I hadn't noticed. "Thanks, Mrs. Woolsey," she said, scurrying off to her next class.

Jamie tried to analyze her panic. *What is happening to me? I'm supposed to be the logical, calm one, and here I am freaking out all over again.* She had to get hold of herself. She had exactly one week to do the portrait now. Jamie wished she could talk with van_gogh, or Coach, or even Bren.

By the time lunch rolled around, Jamie wasn't very hungry, but she took her taco anyway and sat at an empty table.

Amber slid in across from her. "Are you OK, Jamie?"

Jamie sighed. "Not a good day. That's all."

Amber closed her eyes for a minute and bowed her head. The kids around her probably had no idea that she was praying, but Jamie knew. She wished she had that kind of talk-to-me-any-ol'-time relationship with God and Jesus that Amber did. Right now, Jamie would have liked to have a good talk with God about this supposed talent he had supposedly given her.

Bren arrived at their table with the force of a whirlwind. "Why so down, everybody? I love tacos!" She pointed to her food as she rambled. "Ladies and gentlemen, right here on this very plate, we have all the necessary food groups. Cheese for your dairy or milk group. And let's point out our vegetable." She pulled out a piece of shredded lettuce and popped it into her mouth. "Don't forget cow, for the meat group. And tomatoes. Aren't they fruits now? Didn't somebody vote in the tomato as a fruit?"

"Will somebody give this girl an A in food, please?" Amber asked, looking around.

Jamie could see that Bren had no idea she'd upset her in art class. That was good because already Jamie's stupid anger had melted. "Are you going to sit down and eat that stuff or what?" Jamie asked, scooting over and getting some of her appetite back.

"How's your portrait of Emily coming?" Bren asked, setting her tray next to Jamie's.

"It's not. Don't ask," Jamie said.

"When's the contest deadline?" Amber asked.

"A week from today." Jamie and Bren said it at the same time. Jamie was surprised Bren remembered.

"Do you know how to scan in your entry?" Bren asked.

Jamie looked up from her taco. "What? Like I would know how? I was surfing the Web after you jokers logged off last night. I found all kinds of contests. And they all said you had to scan."

"Scanning is pretty easy," Amber said. "You'd just have to take a picture of your portrait, Jamie, and then find a scanner you can use. Maya's mom has one. I'll bet she'd let you use it."

"I'll have to actually have a portrait to scan first," Jamie said. "I really tried to do Emily today. It just wasn't working."

"Well, I love this portrait project thing in art class!" Bren said, her mouth full of taco.

Amber handed her a napkin.

"I have Mark Wellington as a partner," Bren explained to Amber. "He is so much fun! I always thought he was a little strange—well, not strange exactly—quiet, shy. But he's a blast once you get to know him."

Jamie wasn't hungry anymore. She stood up and lifted her tray.

"Don't forget to recycle," Amber said.

"I don't get all this recycling routine," Bren said. "I mean, what happens to all this stuff anyway? I sure don't want to reuse anybody's milk carton or straw. I hate sorting my trash. Gross! I say they ship all of our trash to the Grand Canyon. Dad took us there one summer, and it was really beautiful and all; but basically it's like this big hole in the ground, and we could fit the whole world's garbage in there and never even see it because that canyon is so deep."

Amber rushed to the ecological defense of the Grand Canyon, and Jamie made her getaway. She wished she could just start the whole day over. Jamie's mom was always saying that the teen years were the time to discover who you really were. Mom talked a lot about Christ living inside of you, how you needed to uncover your unique gifts and find out who you really were—just as Jamie was always trying to discover the real portrait as she drew.

Jamie usually tuned Mom out during these mother-daughter talks. She'd always known exactly who she was—Jamie Chandler, artist. Of course she knew herself—except for lately. These days, she barely recognized the sulky Jamie who got upset every time Bren giggled at Mark.

After school, Jamie went straight to the Gnosh to help Mr. Cross with the after-school crowd. It was good to be busy. It kept her mind off her problems. Most of the kids ordered Cokes or fries. A few got ice cream. Maya came by and helped.

Then just like it did on so many other days, the crowd evaporated. "How does that happen?" Jamie asked, stopping for a minute to catch her breath and enjoy the relative quiet of the emptying Gnosh. "Do they all get together and decide to rush us at once and then take off?"

Maya plopped into a chair, her legs stretched straight out in front of her, crossed at the ankles. "It's the same way at the supermarket. Mom claims she always picks the wrong line at the wrong time and waits and waits. Then when she leaves, nobody's in line."

"That reminds me!" Maya pulled herself up in the chair. "Mom said to tell you she'd be glad to help you with your portrait or anything if you need her."

"Tell her thanks, Maya. That's really nice." Dr. Cross had all kinds of degrees in art. She taught at the community college, but she'd had paintings hanging in New York galleries. "Right now I don't see how anybody can help me."

Jamie got a clean sponge and started picking up straw wrappers, clearing glasses, and wiping tables. As she wiped Mark's table, the one he'd sat at with his friends Monday night, Jamie wondered if Mark would ever come back to the Gnosh. Maybe she'd scared him away for good.

Bren and Amber were supposed to drop by after dinner. the Gnosh was filling up again by the time Amber strolled in with

Morgan instead. Amber's honey-blonde hair was soaking wet, pulled back in a ponytail.

"Did you do extra yardage?" Maya yelled from behind the counter.

"Hey!" Amber called back. She headed for their booth. "I just swam for fun," she said, sliding in.

"Sure she did," Morgan teased.

"Where's Bren?" Jamie asked, setting down burgers and fries for a couple of regular senior citizens.

"She was right behind us," Morgan said. "She stopped to talk, I think."

Outside the Gnosh came the unmistakable sound of Bren Mickler's laugh. Jamie smiled to herself and reached back to untie her apron. She hadn't taken a break all afternoon. She was looking forward to hanging out with her friends for a little while. "Bren, I could hear you a mile—" Jamie stopped cold.

Coming through the door was Bren Mickler . . . on the arm of Mark Wellington.

"Jamie! You're here!" Bren cried. "Look what the cat dragged in!" She elbowed Mark, who looked about as uncomfortable as Jamie felt.

Neither Mark nor Jamie spoke, but Bren didn't seem to notice. "You should have been in study hall!" Bren chattered as they walked up to the table. "A spider, a real live spider, ran across my foot! And I screamed, and then the freshmen girls at my study table saw it and went nuts. And then Amanda

Muffet—do you know her? That's her real name—Muffet, as in 'Little Miss Muffet'—I'm not making this up—Amanda screams and tells everyone to stay away and not step on the spider because spiders are our friends and they kill other bugs. And she has fourteen of them as pets and that this one is a female and about to lay eggs!"

Jamie glanced sideways at Mark. He was staring at his shoes and rocking back on his heels.

Bren kept talking as she tugged Mark over to Amber and Morgan. "And then Little Ms. Muffet said that there are billions and billions of spiders in the world, way more than people—which really gives me the creeps. And in one year spiders eat so many bugs that if you stacked them in a huge pile, they'd weigh as much as fifty million people! Or something like that. Maybe it was fifty billion. Anyway, a whole lot of bugs, and a whole bunch of spiders."

Maya brushed past Jamie, who was still standing in front of the door, right where she'd been when Bren made her entrance. "Come on, Jamie!" Maya said. "Break time!" She slid into the booth next to Amber.

"That's OK," Jamie muttered.

"Squeeze us in, Morgan!" Bren cried, pushing her over and pulling Mark beside her, so Bren was in the middle, three on one side.

Bren is such a flirt! Jamie told herself Bren didn't mean to be. She just bubbled—sometimes all over other people. Jamie walked quietly back to the kitchen as she retied her apron. A few minutes later Maya brought the orders back, and Jamie filled them, turning down their pleas for her to sit with them.

Bren was still babbling about spiders when Jamie brought them their drinks. "So, for every acre of land, there are more than two million spiders! But Amanda says house spiders are the only gross ones. They make these kind of hammock webs and eat insects and leaves and spit out little pieces of insects and stuff into their webs."

Jamie knew Bren was just being Bren. *Besides,* she thought as she headed for another table, *Mark and I have nothing going. We've probably said all of two words to each other—and my two words have been I'm sorry. I'm sorry. I'm sorry.*

Mark must have downed his Sprite in one gulp because Jamie hadn't even made it back to the kitchen when she heard him behind her. "'Night, Jamie," he said.

"Don't go, Mark!" Bren yelled across the restaurant.

Mark waved, without turning back to them. Then he left.

Why didn't I at least say good-bye? Jamie wished she had one tenth the conversational powers of Bren Mickler.

"I'm off, too," Amber said. "Test tomorrow."

The others left soon after Amber, and Jamie finished her shift.

Jamie lugged her portfolio and backpack up the steps to her front porch. The house was dark except for TV light coming from the living room.

"We're in here, Jamie!" Mom called.

Canned TV laughter was followed by Jessica's giggle that sounded like soft rain on the roof or puppies scampering up stairs. Jamie would have loved to can Jessica's laugh, save it for moments just like this when she really needed it.

Mom, Jessica, and Jordan were huddled on the couch, munching popcorn and watching a movie Jamie had already seen. They looked like one big, happy family.

"Hi, everybody," Jamie said.

"Shhhh!" Jordan scolded. So much for one big, happy family.

"Can you watch with us, or do you have homework, Jamie?" Mom asked, without turning around.

"I've got homework. And I'm beat. It's OK." Jamie trudged down the hall to her room, flung her pack on her bed and set down her portfolio. Her arms ached. Slumping to the floor, she opened the portfolio and flung back the flap. Maybe tomorrow's art class would go better. Maybe one look at her dad's work would inspire her to do better things the next day.

Jamie felt for the portrait. She looked inside, stuck both hands all around inside the rough leather compartments. It wasn't there. *Jamie's Portrait* was gone!

chapter.9

Jamie searched frantically for the missing portrait. *How could this have happened?* She looked under her bed, in her closet, everywhere, although she knew she'd lost it at school.

It must have fallen out somewhere—at the Gnosh, on the way home, maybe at school or in the gym. Jamie thought of how panic-stricken she'd been when she'd realized she didn't have the portfolio with her in chemistry class. Maybe her panic hadn't been so stupid after all.

She wanted to talk to someone, but not to Mom. Jamie hadn't shown her mother the portrait. She was afraid it would just make her sad, make her remember things she'd worked hard to forget.

Bren? Jamie wasn't exactly mad at Bren, but she didn't feel like confiding in her either. It would have been nice to talk to Coach, but he always considered his evenings at home to be "family night," and she didn't want to bother him.

Unless he's online! Van_gogh!

Jamie didn't check to see if anybody was in TodaysGirls.com chat room. Everybody except Bren was probably doing homework. Instead, Jamie went straight to the Christian Teen Chat Web site and clicked directly to Stranded.

Van_gogh didn't appear in the main dialog box, but he was listed as present in the sidebar box. Jamie clicked on his name, inviting him to a private chat.

rembrandt: i am so glad ur here!!!! need to talk, ok?
van_gogh: thought you might. that's Y i'm here. ??

Jamie filled van_gogh in on everything—finding the portfolio, discovering the portrait her dad had drawn, how wonderful it was, how it had just vanished, and how horrible she felt, although she wasn't even sure why.

rembrandt: i don't know why i should care if i have lost
 it. it's not like i want something to remember my dad
 by.
van_gogh: it's ok to miss your dad, rembrandt.
rembrandt: i don't miss him!!!!!!!!!!!!!!!!!!!
van_gogh: ok. relax. that portrait will turn up FWIW.
rembrandt: u think?

van_gogh: JMO, but u need to focus on that portrait contest!

Jamie told van_gogh about her miserable attempts to capture the soul of Emily Eaton on paper.

rembrandt: i think you have 2 want 2 see inside some-body's soul to capture them in a portrait. u have to want to no what makes them tick.
van_gogh: !!!!!!! Idea!!!!!!!!
rembrandt: am i wrong, or do i get the feeling you have an idea?
van_gogh: rembrandt! u keep saying u wish u could fig-ure yourself out. u want to use the talent God put inside u, right?
rembrandt: right . . . so . . .
van_gogh: do a self-portrait!!!!!!!!!!!!!!!!!!!!

The first thing that popped into Jamie's brain the next morn-ing was the image of all those exclamation points. *Do a self-por-trait!!!!!!!!!!!!!!!!!!*

As Jamie got dressed and washed up, loaded her backpack and portfolio, and downed breakfast, she became more and more convinced that van_gogh was absolutely right. He had come up with the answer. She could do a self-portrait. It wouldn't be easy. She'd have to work like crazy to meet the deadline. But the idea of discovering her own portrait and working it out on paper thrilled her.

She'd have to find a way to start her new portrait project in art class. Time was too crucial to waste that hour on a portrait of Emily. Jamie was so excited about her self-portrait, that she almost forgot about her dad's portrait. And then, for a minute, remembering the loss of *Jamie's Portrait* doused her enthusiasm. But the portrait would turn up. Van_gogh was right. Van_gogh was right about everything!

Jamie's mom dropped her off at school in time for swim practice. Neither of them mentioned the portfolio until Jamie was out of the car. She'd suspected her mom had caught a glimpse of it before now, but neither of them had risked opening old wounds by talking about it.

"Jamie!" Mom called when Jamie was halfway up the sidewalk to school. "The portfolio—it looks good on you!"

Jamie waved. She knew she had just about the best mom in the whole world.

Jamie greeted the swimmers, parked her bags, and stood by Coach to record times. Amber worked the backstroke. Maya did butterfly laps, then freestyle. Morgan started off freestyle and finished working on her breaststroke. Jamie loved to watch them swim. She felt like jumping in the water with them, which is what Bren always goaded her to do.

"Coach," Jamie said, when the others ran to the locker room to change, "you didn't by any chance find a picture around here yesterday, did you?"

"A picture?" He stared at her. "No. Why?"

Jamie shrugged. "Because I lost one."

"I hate that!" Coach said. "The boys lose things all the time. I tell them: 'Look in the last place you plan to search, 'cause that's always where you' find it.' When my wife loses something, I tell her to go look where it should be, in the first place she looked. And nine times out of ten, she finds it. As for me, I never lose anything."

Jamie laughed. "Good advice, Coach. I'll make a note. Never lose anything."

Jamie collected her backpack and portfolio and walked to art class. *Harrison Short is one of a kind,* she thought. Bren kidded him that he had a Napoleon complex, but Jamie never minded taking orders from Coach.

The closer Jamie got to art class, the faster her heart beat. This time nothing would get in her way. She was going to do the most wonderful self-portrait, and she would start it right now.

After checking with Mrs. Woolsey for the lost picture, Jamie set up her easel and waited for Bren to get to class.

"Bren!" Jamie accosted her in the doorway. "Quick! I need to borrow your mirror."

Bren set down her pack and pulled it open. "The big one, the middle-sized, or the little one?" She giggled.

"The tiny one with the clip on the side."

Bren came out with exactly the mirror Jamie needed. "Do

you want any lipstick?" she asked. "I just got this great color, Cantaloupe Melon. It would look so good on you!"

"Nope. Thanks a million, Bren!" Jamie raced for her artist's pad.

"Keep the mirror, Jamie!" Bren called after her.

Jamie set up everything while Emily was still getting out her easel. This time she couldn't wait for Emily to get set up. "Let me help," she offered.

As soon as the easels were back to back, Jamie clipped on the mirror and got to it.

"Hey, you can't start without me!" Emily whined.

Jamie tried not to grin. Her hand moved confidently as she looked from the mirror to the paper and back and forth. As Jamie drew, it was as if she existed inside of a bubble, where none of the classroom distractions could reach her. She tuned out Emily's gripes, Bren's giggles, Mrs. Woolsey's cries. There was nothing except this paper, those lines, and maybe—just maybe—the talent God had given her.

As her charcoal pencil moved faster, something inside of Jamie emptied onto the page and into the portrait. She was drawing her soul, the soul of an artist. They were rough lines, but Jamie could see through them, as if a wonderful portrait already lay beneath the white of the page and she was just uncovering it.

"Five minutes left! Put your materials away!" Mrs. Woolsey shouted.

Jamie could not believe it. The whole class hour had flown

by in a glorious blur. Catching a glimpse of Mrs. Woolsey heading her way, she hurriedly closed her artist's pad. But she wasn't quick enough. Mrs. Woolsey reached over her shoulder and flipped back the cover.

"Hmmmm," said Mrs. Woolsey, her chin held in her hand. "The shape of the head is all wrong, Jamie. I believe you had a better proportion going yesterday in your sketch. It's lovely, but it doesn't look at all like Emily."

"Oh well," Jamie said vaguely.

Mrs. Woolsey reached for Jamie's charcoal pencil. "Let me see if I can help get—"

Jamie snatched back the pencil and flipped her pad closed again. "That's OK. Thank you, Mrs. Woolsey," she said. "I'll give it another try tomorrow." Jamie stopped. "Or better yet, Mrs. Woolsey," she said, before her teacher scooted back to her desk, "would it be alright if I took my art project home to work on after school?" *OK, God. I'm going to try Amber's on-the-spot praying. Please have her say yes!*

Mrs. Woolsey cocked her head to one side. "Oh, I don't know. I don't usually let materials out of the room. Besides, you wouldn't have Emily to look at."

"But I could reshape some of the lines." *Please, please!* Jamie prayed.

Mrs. Woolsey sighed. "Well, maybe if you spray it with the charcoal sealant first . . . I guess it would be alright. Just be careful with it."

"I will!" Jamie cried. She hugged the astonished Mrs. Woolsey. "Thank you!" *And thank you, God.*

Jamie scooped up her pencil, Bren's mirror, and her artist's pad and carried them to her portfolio. She elbowed the flap open and started to drop in her stuff.

Something stopped her. The back pocket of her portfolio bulged. Jamie reached in. There was *Jamie's Portrait.* Jamie stared at it. How could it be there? She remembered Coach's advice to go look again in the place where it should have been. And there it was. Could it possibly have been there all along?

From then on, Jamie worked on her portrait every spare minute. She had never enjoyed anything as much. Thursday night Jordan got into an argument with Mom again when Mom refused to let her go to an overnight party. But Jamie disappeared inside her own world, where she drew, peeling off layer after layer of depth she didn't even know she had.

She hadn't heard a thing until a little voice said, "Jamie, it's beautiful! It looks just like you." Jessica, in a flowered flannel nightgown, stood beside Jamie, staring at the portrait.

"Oh, Jess," Jamie said, "you can't tell anybody!"

"Why? It's so good!" Jessica seemed hypnotized by the portrait.

Jamie wasn't even sure herself why she didn't want anyone to see her portrait until it was finished, not until it hung proudly at the art show. She wouldn't tell her friends about the portrait and her plans to enter the Interlochen contest until the contest was all over. Probably, she admitted, she was afraid of losing, afraid of disappointing them or having them feel sorry for her.

"Don't you want to show Mom?" Jessica pressed.

"NO! And you can't tell her either."

"Mom said you didn't want us to see whatever you were working on in here," Jessica said. "She said Daddy was the same way. He never let her see anything he was drawing or painting until it was hanging in an art gallery."

Jamie was surprised. Mom never talked to her about Dad. Maybe Jessica asked so many questions, Mom had to answer some of them.

"This is really important, Jessica," Jamie said, putting one hand on Jessica's shoulder and staring into her eyes. "This has to be our secret, OK?"

Jessica sighed. "OK. It's just so beautiful. You look just like an artist in it."

Jamie gave her sister a hug. "Jess, that is the nicest thing anybody ever said to me."

Friday in class Jamie set up her easel. She still had a long way to go. The deadline was Wednesday at noon, but she'd have to photograph the portrait and scan it into the computer before then.

"Class," Mrs. Woolsey shouted. "Our art show is just around the corner! I expect everybody to work hard today."

Jamie was already hard at work. She needed to rework the

hairline and detail the hair. And she hadn't decided what to do about the neckline and collar.

At the end of class, she was so intent on her drawing that she didn't even notice Emily had left her side of the easels and sneaked around behind Jamie.

"Mrs. Woolsey!" cried Emily. "Come and see! Look what Jamie's done! That's not me! Her portrait looks like her!"

chapter.10

J amie tried to seal the portrait and get it into her portfolio, but she wasn't quick enough. And Emily wouldn't
let up.

"You have to see this, Mrs. Woolsey!" Emily cried.

The rest of the class was packing up and filtering out of the room.
Jamie shoved her portrait the rest of the way inside her portfolio and
closed the flap. "Emily's right," she said.

"See? Told you!" Emily said smugly.

"You know, I've had so much trouble getting Emily's proportions right, I probably should start from scratch."

"But it's so late, Jamie," Mrs. Woolsey said. "The art show—"

"I'll have something for the art show, Mrs. Woolsey," Jamie
insisted. "I promise."

"Well," she said, staring at Jamie's portfolio as if she could see through it to the portrait, "I guess that's what's important now. I'll see if I can help you more with your new one."

"Thanks," Jamie said. That was close! Jamie knew she couldn't bring her self-portrait to art class again. She'd have to work on it at home. But she couldn't help feeling a little proud. Even Emily had recognized her in the unfinished portrait.

The weekend flew by. Even though Saturday was the busiest day at the Gnosh Pit, Mr. Cross agreed to let Jamie come in late. She hadn't even explained why. Maya and Morgan were lucky to have a dad like that, and a great mom, too.

Jamie worked on her drawing all morning and then raced to the Gnosh. When she walked in, Dr. Cross was sitting at the counter eating ice cream. She even made that an event, methodically easing the long spoon into the parfait glass and gracefully coming out with exactly the right amount. Catherine Cross always made Jamie think of an actress or a model. She wore a straight brown-and-orange patterned silk dress that could have been a painting in anybody else's house. The design looked original, like a modern art masterpiece. Her gold necklace and bracelet looked Mayan.

"Well, Jamie, how are you?" Dr. Cross sounded genuinely happy to see her.

"OK, I guess," Jamie answered.

"I was hoping I'd run into you. How's your art coming? Morgan said something about a contest you were entering?"

"Yeah, if I can get it done in time."

"Well, you let me know if I can help in any way." It was a great offer coming from her. Everybody Jamie knew from the community college said Catherine Cross was the best teacher there. She'd left a teaching job at NYU, just so she could raise her kids out of the city.

"Thanks a lot, Dr. Cross," Jamie said. Then she got an idea. "I do have something you maybe could help me with."

"Anything," Dr. Cross said.

Jamie hadn't had much time to worry about details of her contest entry. She'd used every ounce of worry up on the portrait itself. "Dr. Cross," she started, "if I get everything done in time, I still need to have the picture scanned onto a disk so I can send it in to the contest."

"Not a problem," she answered. "We have a great scanner in my office at school. Just let me know, and I'll be there to help."

Jamie thanked her. The pieces were coming together. Now all she had to do was finish her portrait in time.

"Hi, Jamie."

Jamie turned around, and there was Mark. He had his hands in his pockets and a grin that came from his eyes more than from his mouth.

"Hi," Jamie said back. *Great conversation, Jamie!*

They stood toe-to-toe without speaking for what seemed like minutes to Jamie. Then Mark nodded and walked to "his" table and sat down.

"I think someone has been looking for you," Dr. Cross whispered.

Jamie wheeled around, and Dr. Cross winked. "What?" Jamie whispered back.

"That poor boy has been by here three times this morning. This is the first time he's taken a seat."

Jamie could feel her face heat up. "No way," she said.

"Hmmmm." Dr. Cross went back to her ice cream.

Jamie tied on her apron and walked to Mark to take his order. "What can I get you?" she asked, hating the sound of her stiff, thin voice.

"Uh . . . a Sprite?" he said.

"OK," she said, waiting.

"That's all . . . if that's OK," he added quickly.

"Yeah! That's OK. That's good," Jamie said.

"Good," Mark said.

"Good."

Jamie rolled her eyes up at the ceiling as she took his order to the kitchen. If Mark had been coming by to see her, he wouldn't make that mistake again. Why couldn't she think of something clever to say, like Bren?

She was surprised to find Mr. Cross at the grill. "Where's Maya?" Jamie asked.

"Swim practice," he answered. "Harry called them in this morning for an extra workout. Morgan told him you were probably too busy to help."

Maybe Jamie could get her life back to normal after the contest and the art show—whatever normal was.

"Jamie," Dr. Cross called in from her seat at the counter, "why don't you take a break and sit with your friend for a few minutes?"

"Take a break?" Mr. Cross shouted back. "She just got here!"

"I'll cover for her," coaxed his wife.

Mr. Cross sighed. "Take five, Jamie."

"Thanks!"

Mr. Cross handed Jamie two Sprites. "Since you've worked up such a big thirst already," he teased.

Jamie took both Sprites to Mark's table. "I'm on break, Mark," she said, her voice shaking. "Could I join you? Unless you—"

"Yes!" Mark said. He pulled a chair back for her. "Great!"

They unwrapped straws together and sipped their Sprites.

"So, how's your portrait coming?" Mark asked at last.

"Haven't you heard Emily complain?" Jamie said. "She thinks it's pretty bad."

"Emily doesn't like anybody's work except her own. I'll bet yours is great."

Jamie shrugged. "How about yours?"

Mark shook his head. "Mine looks more like a moving picture. Bren doesn't hold still for more than two seconds at a time. Nate says mine looks like a Halloween witch with a ponytail."

They laughed. Jamie could feel her tension drain. "Bren doesn't need to hear that. She'd freak! Who's Nate?"

"My brother," Mark explained. "He's in your sister's class."

"Jessica's?" Jamie asked.

"My brother says Jessica is a brain. Nate's not exactly an ace at school, but I wouldn't trade him for anything."

"I know what you mean," Jamie said. She liked that Mark obviously loved his little brother. Most guys talked like they hated their siblings and parents. She had to admit that although she sometimes felt like strangling Jordan, when she got right down to it, she wouldn't have traded her family for anything either.

"I better get back," Jamie said.

"Me too," he said, getting up and leaving half of his Sprite on the table.

Sunday, Jamie hardly had any time to work on her portrait. Church and the food drive took up most of the day. Monday morning came, and Jamie hadn't gotten nearly as far on her picture as she'd hoped. She'd need to work right up to the wire to pull it off by Tuesday. She kept changing her mind on a collar and neckline. And she knew she couldn't risk taking the portrait to art class again.

"Starting over at this late date, Jamie?" Mrs. Woolsey asked, hovering as usual.

"I think it's best," Jamie said, glad she'd left her self-portrait at home.

"Try to get it right this time," Emily whispered as soon as Mrs. Woolsey waddled away. "There's no way you can get it done in time for Interlochen's deadline."

Jamie drew fast, almost without thinking. Her mind was visualizing the way she wanted her neck in the self-portrait. What if she couldn't get it done in time?

Emily kept chattering as she finished her portrait. "I'm taking my portrait home tonight so my father can photograph it with his digital camera. I can download it and e-mail it to Interlochen in plenty of time."

Jamie tried not to let Emily know that she was getting to her. What if Jamie couldn't get the portrait photographed and scanned in time?

Tuesday afternoon came and Jamie still hadn't finished her self-portrait. On the walk home from school, she tried on-the-spot praying again. *God, this is it. I'm going to trust you to help me finish my portrait. Amen.*

When Jamie picked up her pencil, it felt as if it melded into her finger bones. Her drawing began to flow from inside her like blood from her veins. As she worked on the neckline that had resisted her all week, Jamie could almost feel the tickle on her own neck.

The page filled itself with her portrait, lines fitting into spaces she hadn't noticed before. Even the suggestion of collar seemed to come from somewhere else. There was nothing like it in Jamie's closet. She didn't remember having seen a blouse or dress like it. But the collar appeared under her pencil just the same, as if no other item of clothing in the entire world could have gone there. And when the pencil stopped, there was no doubt in Jamie's mind. Her portrait was finished.

"That's it!" she exclaimed out loud, stepping back from her portrait. This was Jamie the Artist staring back at her, brimming with confidence, dedication, and artistic talent.

Jamie glanced at the clock and couldn't believe it was six already. "Jordan!" she yelled, bursting in on her sisters. "Can I use your camera?"

"This film is expensive, Jamie," Jordan said, slipping her headphones from her ears to her neck.

"Please, Jordan!" Jamie pleaded. "I finished my contest portrait! But I have to get a picture of it!"

"When's the deadline?" Jordan asked.

"Tomorrow noon. But if I can get a photo of it right now, Dr. Cross said she'd scan it and send it to the contest site for me in the morning before school."

"Then you better hurry!" Jordan said, running to her dresser and getting her camera. "Twelve pictures left. Is that enough? Go take the whole roll!"

"We can go to PictureThis!" Jessica shouted. "Hurry!"

Jamie's mother came to the doorway. "What's going on?"

Jamie filled her mother in as fast as she could.

"We can do this if we all hurry!" Mom said. "I'll go start the car. And I'll call Dr. Cross to make sure she'll be in her office before school."

Jamie was touched by the teamwork—all for her. "Thanks!" she yelled. In her room, she took photos of her self-portrait from a variety of angles and distances, moving the lights into different positions and clicking until she'd used the rest of Jordan's film. Then they all piled into the car.

Mom wheeled into the drive-thru at PictureThis and handed the film through the customer window. "Take good care of these!" she said. "We need them in an hour."

"Sorry," said the heavyset, gray-haired woman, who looked tired of her job and even more tired of the little duck-billed PictureThis cap they made her wear. "Busy night. Tomorrow alright? About noon?"

"No!" Jessica shrieked. "This is important! It's for my sister, the artist!"

The woman peered in the backseat at Jessica, who was on the verge of tears. "Well, in that case," said the woman, "I guess I better give this roll priority handling! Come back in an hour."

Mom treated them to root beer floats. They picked up a few things at the grocery store. And they still got back to PictureThis fifteen minutes early. They went inside and stepped to the back of a long line.

"Priority call!" The woman who had waited on them was

waving a white packet in their direction. "Chandlers come to the front, please!"

Jamie got her pictures and thanked the woman. *Thank you, too, God,* she prayed as they walked to the car, the pack of photos clutched to her chest. If she was going to ask for stuff on the spot, the least she could do was thank God on the spot.

She could hardly wait to peek at the pictures, but she didn't want anyone else to see them. It would be as awful as anyone seeing her portrait before the time was perfect. She fastened her seat belt and turned on the overhead light.

"Let me see!" Jessica cried.

"You know better than that," Mom said. "An artist never shows her art until it's properly displayed. We'll all see it at the art show on Saturday. Right, Jamie?"

"Thanks, Mom," Jamie whispered.

"No fair!" Jordan cried. "It's my film! I should get to see the pictures now!"

Jamie handed Jordan several pictures her sister must have taken at the mall. Most of them were pictures of boys—boys stuffing down French fries, boys running up a down escalator, boys making stupid faces.

"Tell you what, Jordan," Jamie said as Mom drove home. "You don't have to show Mom your photos, and I don't have to show you mine."

chapter.11

Next morning the whole family—even Jordan—rode along to the college to meet Dr. Cross. Jessica didn't say a word about the possibility of being late to school.

Jamie took her best photo to Dr. Cross's office while Mom and the girls waited in the car. "Thanks for doing this," she said as Dr. Cross turned on the scanner.

"Glad to do it, Jamie," she said. "Just give me the photograph, and I'll stick it in here."

Jamie hesitated. "I hate to ask you this, but is there any way I could do it myself?"

"You are truly an artist, Jamie Chandler," Dr. Cross said, grinning. "So am I. I know exactly how you feel." Turning her back on the scanner, Dr. Cross told Jamie what to do.

It wasn't much harder than photocopying and worked as

quickly. Jamie pulled up the picture to a blank screen, gave it a title, *Jamie's Self-Portrait,* and saved it to a blank disk. Then she sent the image to the designated Interlochen page and prayed as she walked to the car. Now all she could do was wait.

Waiting turned out to be the hardest thing Jamie had ever done. She knew the winner wouldn't be announced until Friday morning, but the first thing she did when she got home from school was to check the Interlochen Web page just in case. She checked again after work and then again first thing the following morning. She found the same message she'd read the last two days: Contest results Friday.

In art class on Thursday, Jamie kept working on her portrait of Emily.

"Now that is coming along nicely, Jamie," Mrs. Woolsey said, peering over Jamie's shoulder. "It looks just like Emily . . . except for that mouth."

"It doesn't matter how good your portrait is," Emily said when Mrs. Woolsey was gone. "You missed the Interlochen deadline."

Jamie thought she'd burst inside, but she held her tongue.

After working at the Gnosh for only an hour, Jamie went home and turned on her computer. Five o'clock—right on schedule for the TodaysGirls.com chat room. It was nice to have more time with her friends. Now that she didn't have to spend so much time drawing, she could work on her part of the Web site, the Artist's Corner. Maybe she could display her self-portrait there.

Jamie typed in the address: TodaysGirls.com, and her password: Jamie003. She had a sense of coming home as she entered the chat room.

faithful1: kewl! GR8 to have u back! :)

jellybean: how r u doing?

rembrandt: GR8 to b back. doing ok. u looked GR8 @ swim practice, faithful1. u all did!

nycbutterfly: thanx! we better or coach will have r heads!

jellybean: wish you could come with us tomorrow to the meet!

rembrandt: me 2! i promised Mrs. W. I'd help set up for the art show. would rather be with u.

jellybean: Mom said Mark was @ the Gnosh looking for you.

rembrandt: he was?

nycbutterfly: kewl!

faithful1: is something going on that i don't know about????????

rembrandt: LOL!! Mark is awfully nice.

jellybean: well so r u!!!

rembrandt: where's chicChick anyway? i thought she'd

be here for sure!

nycbutterfly: that's what i'd like to know! she's always here!

faithful1: chicChick was in the chat room when I logged on. said she'd BRB.

nycbutterfly: probably got held up chatting somewhere! LOL.

It felt great for Jamie to relax in the security of their own chat room and talk about nothing and everything with her friends. She felt guilty for keeping her portrait a secret from them, but she hoped they'd understand. If she'd had more confidence—in herself, in the talent God had given her—she probably would have told them all along. Maybe next time she would. And if she won, they'd be so surprised, they'd have to forgive her.

Finally Bren made her grand entrance. The line read:

chicChick has entered the room

faithful1: welcome queen of chat!

nycbutterfly: ditto! where've u been??

chicChick: is rembrandt here?

rembrandt: i'm here. been waiting for u.

chicChick: get out of here now! go!!!!

faithful1: what r u talking about?

chicChick: hold the fone! hold everything! go directly to Interlochen Web site! they've announced the winners!

The winners? Already? But they weren't supposed to post winners until tomorrow morning. Jamie's hands trembled as she exited the chat room and typed in the address for the Interlochen site. It seemed to take forever for her screen to get the message. Her heart raced as she watched the bytes add up, then empty out.

Finally the screen flipped to Interlochen's home page. She waited as the logo of the school appeared at the top of the screen. Then the picture of the campus took shape, filling the top half of the screen.

"Come on!" Jamie muttered, willing the computer to work faster.

The sidebar came in clearly, and the words *Contest results!* flashed on and off. Jamie took a deep breath and clicked on the *click here* symbol.

A box appeared in the middle of the screen, labeled: "This year's winner of the Interlochen Aspiring Artists Award."

And beneath that line was the name of the winner: Jamie Chandler.

"I won! I won!" Jamie raced to the hall, shouting at the top of her lungs. "I won the scholarship!"

Mom came running down the hall. Jordan and Jessica tore out of their rooms, and they all met in the middle, jumping and hugging, and cheering.

"I knew it!" Jordan yelled. "Way to go, sister!"

Jamie's mom was crying. "I am so proud of you, Jamie!"

Jessica, in her own quiet way, hugged her sister and whispered, "You really are an artist."

Friday morning Jamie got up and checked the Interlochen Web site to be sure she hadn't just dreamed that she won. Then she clicked over to the message board at the Christian Teen Chat center and left a note for van_gogh: thanks, van_gogh. I won!!!!

thanks for encouraging me. don't know what i would have done without u! rembrandt

Jamie was so excited she completely forgot about the swim meet and arrived early to school. Her best friends wouldn't even be at school the whole day. She went straight to her locker and couldn't believe what she found. Streamers covered the door. A big sign read: JAMIE CHANDLER IS A WINNER!!!! GR8! WTG, Jamie!!!!

Inside her locker, the girls had stuffed Ping-Pong balls. They exploded into the hall, bouncing in all directions. On the inside of the door was a note. Jamie read it: "Congratulations from TodaysGirls.com! Meet us at the Gnosh at 7 tonight!" By the time she'd collected all of the Ping-Pong balls, it was almost time for art class. She trapped them back inside her locker and slammed the door.

Jamie left the sign up on her locker and walked to art class, almost afraid she'd wake up and this would all be a dream. By the time she reached her classroom, a dozen kids had congratulated her. Bren must have been on the phone all night telling everybody.

"Congratulations, Jamie!" cried Mrs. Woolsey as soon as Jamie walked in. "We are so proud of you! Interlochen is a wonderful school! Did I tell you I used to have a beau who went there?"

Jamie nodded.

"Well, we'll set up your portrait in the center position at the art show, right where people walk in. I've called the media and—"

"The media?" Jamie asked.

"Well, you know, the *Edgewood Times*. They want to come and take your picture beside the winning portrait."

Emily Eaton had been standing behind Mrs. Woolsey. She leaned around her, "What did you call it anyway?" she said. "*Emily's Portrait*? I don't get it. It wasn't even finished in time for the deadline."

"Actually, I did another portrait, a self-portrait," Jamie admitted.

"I knew it!" Emily cried. "See, Mrs. Woolsey? I told you she was doing a portrait of herself! That wasn't fair!"

"Well, what counts is that you won," Mrs. Woolsey said absently.

Mark came up to Jamie. She was glad to see him. "Congratulations, Jamie!" He grasped her right arm in his hand. Jamie was sure he held on to it much longer than necessary.

"Thanks, Mark," she managed.

"I bet your whole family's going crazy," he said.

Jamie grinned. "Pretty much."

"Let's finish those portraits, class!" cheered Mrs. Woolsey. "Tomorrow is the art show, and we must get all set up. Be sure to bring your families."

Jamie worked on her portrait of Emily and finished it by the end of the hour. It wasn't half bad, as far as a likeness of her subject went, although Emily still insisted the mouth was too big.

After school she and Mark worked together setting up bulletin boards for the backs of the show tables and arranging the partitions, while Emily and Mrs. Woolsey put up signs.

"I want everyone here early tomorrow morning!" Mrs. Woolsey yelled. "We'll set up the portraits and sculptures then. I don't want them sitting out overnight."

"This is a great spot," Mark said as Jamie straightened the easel that would hold her winning portrait the next morning. "You deserve it."

"Thanks, Mark."

Jamie had just enough time to hurry home, make spaghetti, and eat a quick supper with her family. It was nice. They'd all shared in her victory, and she wanted them to share in the glory on Saturday.

A little before seven, Jamie took off on foot for the Gnosh. An evening chill blew in with the wind, making the treetops sway. She couldn't wait to see her friends at the Gnosh. She wanted to fill them in on all the details—on how she'd decided to try a self-portrait, how she almost hadn't made the deadline, why she'd kept it a secret, everything.

It felt weird going to the Gnosh when she didn't have to work, but there was no place on earth she'd rather be right now than with her friends.

Jamie walked up the drive to the restaurant. It should have been a busy hour, but there was none of the usual Friday night frenzy coming from inside. She opened the door and couldn't believe no one was there. No one! "Hello?" she called.

She didn't even see Mr. Cross or the cook in the kitchen. "Hello?" she called louder. "Is anybody here?"

"Surprise!" "Surprise!" "Surprise!"

Heads popped up from behind the counter. They were all there—Maya, Morgan, their parents, Amber, Bren, several kids from their art class, and even a couple of people Jamie didn't recognize. "Congratulations, Jamie!" Dr. Cross said, giving her a kiss on the forehead.

Mr. Cross came out of the kitchen carrying a big sheet cake. It was decorated with a paintbrush and artist's pallet, and it read: "Congratulations, Jamie!"

Jamie couldn't speak. It was all she could do not to cry. "I—I—I never expected this," she stammered.

Bren put an arm around her shoulder and led Jamie to a booth. "That's why they call it a surprise party. Get it?" They slid in across from each other while Maya and Morgan helped cut the cake.

"So how was the swim meet?" Jamie asked.

"Cool!" Bren said. "Amber won first, of course. And Maya won first in butterfly. Morgan did great, too. And I had fun!"

Mr. Cross brought each of them a piece of cake, and Amber brought them a pitcher of Diet Coke.

"This is too much," Jamie said, stuffing a big bite of chocolate cake in her mouth.

"I knew all along you'd win!" Bren said, her mouth full and her upper lip smeared with white frosting. "You just didn't have enough confidence in yourself. I was sure you'd have something great to enter in the contest, even though you kept saying nothing was good enough. I hope you're not mad at me."

"Mad at you? Why?" Jamie remembered how mad she'd been—for no good reason—when Bren had walked into the Gnosh with Mark. But she was sure Bren hadn't even noticed.

"Well, I mean, you know, mad at me for being sneaky like that. But I just knew it was the only way to get you into the contest. And it all worked out just like I knew it would."

Bren wasn't making sense, even for Bren. "What do you mean, 'sneaky'?" Jamie asked.

"I mean like sneaking into your portfolio before art class and taking the portrait and everything. I got it back as soon as I could and I took really great care of it. I just had it long enough to take the photos with my dad's digital camera. Then I put—"

"You? You took the portrait?" Jamie asked.

"Yeah, duh!" Bren said. "And even I could see it was plenty good enough to enter in that art contest."

Jamie's chest hurt. Her head was starting to throb.

"You just didn't have the confidence, Jamie. So I went ahead and had Dad scan in the entry a week ago, without telling you, just in case you tried to talk me out of it."

"You entered—" Jamie could barely breathe.

"Did you see it?" Bren asked, downing another bite of cake. "They posted the portrait at the Interlochen site just tonight. It looks awesome!"

"No!" Jamie pushed out of the booth and ran out of the Gnosh. *It can't be! It can't be! It can't be!*

chapter.12

"Y ou're home early," Mom said as Jamie barged into the house without slowing down. "Jamie, is everything alright?"

Jamie didn't answer. She ran to her room and slammed the door. Then she turned on her computer and waited, barely breathing until it warmed up.

Clicking her way into the Web, Jamie stopped on Interlochen's site, clicked on Contest Results again, and waited, the sick feeling growing inside of her. This time her name appeared at the top of the screen. Then the words *Jamie's Portrait*. And beneath that, for all the world to see, was her dad's watercolor.

Jamie slammed her hand on her desk. "No! Not yours! My portrait won! Not yours!"

Friday night Jamie lay in bed and stared at her black ceiling, splashed with moonlight from her window. Every shadow looked like her dad's portrait, the curve he'd given the hairline, the way his lines folded into each other. She shut her eyes and pulled the pillow over her head, but it didn't stop the images marching through her brain. *Jamie's Portrait* loomed behind her closed eyelids.

Something creaked, and she sat up straight in bed. *Go to sleep!* she told herself. The toilet flushed down the hall, and Jamie heard the patter of Jessica's little feet returning to her room.

Jamie curled into a ball under her covers, but the portrait was there, too. Her clock ticked so loudly she wondered how she had ever slept even one minute in this room. She tried not to think, but her mind raced on without her. *How could I have been so stupid? My portrait win a contest? I should have known better! Jamie Chandler has never won anything in her whole life. And wouldn't you know it would be my own father who beat me out!*

She would have laughed at the irony if she hadn't been crying.

What on earth was she going to do now? How could she tell everybody that there had been a mistake? They were all so proud of her. How could she tell Interlochen, her mother, her friends, even Mrs. Woolsey?

And why should she? What difference did it make? It should have been her portrait that won. And in a way, *Jamie's Portrait* really was hers. What would her dad do anyway with a scholarship to an aspiring young artists' camp—even if they could ever track him down to tell him?

He would never know. Nobody would ever know.

It wasn't as if she'd planned the whole thing or even known about it. And if anybody ever needed a scholarship to Interlochen, it was Jamie Chandler.

By the time Jamie got out of bed Saturday morning, she had herself convinced. She'd keep her mouth shut. *Jamie's Portrait* had won, and Jamie was going to take the victory.

Not wanting to talk with her mom over breakfast, Jamie took a granola bar and her portfolio and headed for the park.

"We'll see you at the art show, honey," Mom said. "I'll drop your sisters off and get there as soon as I can."

Outside, the sun was already bright. Instead of going straight to school, Jamie stopped at the park and ate her breakfast on a park bench while families trickled into the playground area. A few feet away, a dad was playing catch with his daughter. Each time she missed it, her dad yelled, "Almost, honey! Good try!"

Jamie couldn't remember her dad ever doing that with her. But they'd shared something—maybe the talent God had given them. *I wish God had given me more, and maybe him less,* Jamie Thought. Even that wasn't fair. Maybe going along with *Jamie's Portrait* evened the score a little. Her dad owed her that much at least, didn't he? She'd go through with this, get to Interlochen, and develop her own talent.

She sat there for a long time, watching the kids go down the slide. When she glanced at her watch, she did a double take. The judging was scheduled to begin in twenty minutes.

Jamie ran the rest of the way to the high school. Mrs. Woolsey was standing at the door waiting for her. "There you are!" she exclaimed. "Everybody has been looking for you!"

"Jamie!" Jordan and two of her friends met her. "Mom would have freaked! Where've you been?"

"You have to get set up!" Jessica said, tugging on Jamie's arm.

Jamie walked to her display table, which sat a foot higher than everybody else's. Mrs. Woolsey trailed behind her. "You have to get that lovely portrait up, dear! The judges will be by any minute. Let me go find that newspaper reporter again."

Jamie's portrait of Emily leaned against the wall, but the big, empty easel was set in front of the table, waiting for Jamie's portrait. She opened her portfolio. Her self-portrait was still inside. She stared at it for a few seconds. It wasn't bad. In fact it might even have been pretty good—just not good enough, not as good as Dad's.

Jamie reached past her self-portrait and pulled out *Jamie's Portrait.* She set it up on the easel and stared at it, struck with the childlike innocence staring back, just as it had the first time she'd found it.

I'm not so innocent anymore, she thought.

"Nice picture!" said Mr. Kistler, the chemistry teacher. "It looks kind of like you."

"Thank you, Mr. Kistler," Jamie said. Each compliment felt

like a hammer landing on her chest, hammering down something inside of her, making her feel worse and worse.

"Jamie?"

Jamie looked down at her little sister, who was squinting hard at *Jamie's Portrait*. "Hi, Jess," she said.

Jessica cocked her head to one side, then the other. "I liked it the other way better," she said.

"You did?" Jamie asked, something fluttering around her heart.

"Yeah, you don't look so much like a real artist in this one," Jessica said. "No offense," she added quickly.

Mark appeared by Jessica's side. He'd brought his little brother with him. "I thought it would look different, too," he said quietly.

Jamie felt the tears spout up from somewhere deep inside.

"Jamie!" Bren said. She and Amber and Maya and Morgan ran up to the easel. "What's the matter? Pull yourself together, girl! The judges are coming!" Bren kept looking down the aisle of tables. "They're almost here!"

"This is so wrong!" Jamie muttered. She knelt down and hugged Jessica. "I'm sorry, Jess. I don't want to disappoint you, but I can't do this."

"Are you alright?" Amber asked.

This was what Jamie had wanted more than anything in the world: the attention, the recognition, a chance to go to an exclusive art camp in the summer. It was her dream.

But not this way.

Mark bent down and whispered, "Come on, Rembrandt. Trust yourself and trust that talent God gave you."

Jamie looked up at Mark, who was smiling a very Van_gogh grin. "You?" she whispered. And the pieces fell into place. She glanced back into Jessica's big brown eyes filled with childlike faith. "You know what, Jess," Jamie said, "you are one smart Chandler!"

"I am?" Jessica asked seriously.

"She really is!" Mark's little brother agreed.

Jamie got her portfolio from behind the table and took it to the easel. With one move, she took down her father's *Jamie's Portrait* and put up her own self-portrait.

Jamie heard Mark say to Jessica, "Your sister is one smart Chandler, too."

"Yeah! That's the one!" Jessica cried, as Jamie straightened her charcoal and the judges stopped in front of her table.

"Not bad, Rembrandt," Mark whispered to Jamie.

"Worthy of Van_gogh?" she whispered back.

"Without a doubt," he answered.

"Will somebody tell me what's going on?" Bren cried.

"I'll explain it all later," she told the girls.

They nodded and didn't ask another question, as if they knew she couldn't answer them now. Jamie knew they'd understand. They were the best friends anybody could ever have.

"We'll catch up with you after the show," Maya said.

"And I have to go get my toothpicks in order!" Bren said, scurrying to her table at the very back of the auditorium.

Three judges passed Jamie's table and gave long looks at the self-portrait. Mom and Coach both came by and praised the portrait. Jamie felt better than she'd felt since discovering the wrong portrait posted on the Interlochen Web site.

"So what are you going to do about Interlochen?" Mark asked.

"I'll e-mail them as soon as I get home and tell them the truth. I'll just withdraw from the contest."

"Can't be easy giving that up, Jamie," Mark said.

"You're telling me?" Jamie said. Giving up that art scholarship would be just about the hardest thing she'd ever done. "I'll get there someday, and I'll get there on my own talent."

"Did you say you were withdrawing from the Interlochen contest?" Emily sneaked out from behind her table, where she'd obviously been eavesdropping. "I knew it! I knew you'd cheated. I just didn't know how. Well, thanks a lot for ruining it for the rest of us!"

Mark reached back to Jamie's table and picked up her classroom portrait of Emily. "Nice portrait," he said, studying it. "Only one problem—I think you got Emily's mouth a little small."

"Very funny, Mark," Emily said, turning her back on him and walking to the front of Jamie's booth. She picked up the self-portrait, held it in both hands, and frowned at it.

"Congratulations! You won!" A tall, red-headed woman, with a ribbon that identified her as "Judge," leaned down and shook Emily's hand. "I guess I'm the first to congratulate you," she said.

"Aren't they going to announce it over the speakers?" Emily asked.

Jamie watched Emily's expression. She didn't look the least bit surprised by her victory, or the least bit grateful.

The speakers around the auditorium whined and squawked. Then the voice of the principal came over the PA system. "Ladies and gentlemen, we have the results of today's art contest. First, we would like to thank all of you for your hard work."

"Yeah, yeah, yeah," Emily muttered. "Get on with it."

Jamie glanced at Mark, and he grinned back at her. She felt dizzy from the roller coaster of emotions—winning, losing, finding out Mark was Van_gogh.

The principal named the judges and asked for applause for them. "And now," he said as a hush fell over the room, "first prize in the Edgewood Art Show goes to . . . Jamie Chandler!"

"What?" Emily cried. She let go of Jamie's portrait as if it were on fire.

Mark dove and caught the portrait before it hit the floor.

Emily kept screaming, "No! There's been a mistake! A horrible mistake!"

"You mean . . ." The red-haired judge looked around for help. "You're not Jamie?"

"Are you kidding?" Emily wailed.

"She's Jamie," Mark said, pointing, then putting the portrait back up on the easel.

Emily ran crying from the auditorium. Amber and Maya and the others rushed up and hugged Jamie, while flashbulbs went off all around her. Shouts of congratulations came from every direction. The judges crowded in and shook her hand.

Jamie searched the crowd through her tears and saw Mark and Jessica standing, one on each side of the portrait—her portrait—one piece of art in what she knew would be a long line of artwork from Jamie the Artist.

Epilogue

Monday night came and found Jamie in deep dialog at TodaysGirls.com.

faithful1: so what did Interlochen say when you told them?

rembrandt: they were so kewl!!! i told them the whole truth.

chicChick: it's all my fault! i never should have gone behind your back like that. 4give me, rembrandt?

rembrandt: for the millionth time, yes! besides, they sent me this GR8 email back from the head of the art camp and one of the instructors.

jellybean: what did they say?

rembrandt: they said they saw a fresh talent in my self-portrait. they loved my "vision" and the "soulish quality."

nycbutterfly: that's so awesome! i love that!

rembrandt: and they told me some points to work on over the summer and invited me to enter the contest again next year!

jellybean: kewl!

faithful1: you did the right thing, rembrant. I'm proud of you. God is proud of u 2.

nycbutterfly: way to go, rembrandt! Mom said she'd be glad to help you, too.

rembrandt: tell her thanx!

chicChick: and u can use your prize money from the art show for materials, rembrandt! that was so kewl, beating Emily in the art show! u deserved it!

rembrandt: thanks, guys! u r the best! and Todays-Girls.com is the best place in the whole world!

chicChick: RO! i could just stay here all night tonight, couldn't u, rembrandt?

rembrandt: oops--sorry. no can do tonight, chicChick. I'm expected @ the Gnosh.

nycbutterfly: i didn't think you were working tonight???

chicChick: ditto! what's the scene @ the Gnosh, rembrandt?

rembrandt: the scene? i guess you could call it artistic-- "Rembrandt meets Van_gogh."

Net Ready, Set Go!

I hope my words and thoughts please you.
Psalm 19:14

The characters of TodaysGirls.com chat online in the safest—and maybe most fun—of all chat rooms! They've created their own private Web site and room! Many Christian teen sites allow you to create your own private chat rooms, and there are other safe options.

Work with your parents to develop a list of safe, appropriate chat rooms. Earn Internet freedom by showing them you can make the right choices. *Honor your father and your mother. . . Deuteronomy 5:16*

Before entering a chat room, you'll select a user name. Although you can use your real name, a nickname is safer. Most people choose one that says something about who they are, like Amber's name, faithful1. Don't be discouraged if the name you select is already taken. You can use a similar one by adding a number at its end.

No one will notice your grammar in a chat room. Don't worry if you spell something wrong or forget to capitalize. Some people even misspell words on purpose. You might see a sentence like How R U?

But sometimes it's important to be accurate. Web site and e-mail addresses must be exact. Pay close attention to whether letters are upper or lowercase. Remember that Web site addresses don't use some punctuation marks, such as hyphens and apostrophes. (That's why the "Today's" in TodaysGirls.com has no apostrophe!) And instead of spaces between words, underlines are used to_make_a_space. And sometimes words just run together like onebigword.

Portrait of Lies

When you're in a chat room, remember real people are typing the words that appear on your screen. Treat them with the same respect you expect from them. Don't say anything you wouldn't want repeated in Sunday school. *Do for other people what you want them to do for you. Luke 6:31*

Sometimes people say mean, hurtful things—things that make us angry. This can happen in chat rooms too. In some chat rooms, you can highlight a rude person's name and click a button that says, "ignore," which will make his or her comments disappear from your screen. You always have the option to switch rooms or sign off. If a particular person becomes a continual problem, or if someone says something especially vicious, you should report this problem user to the chat service. *Ask God to bless those who say bad things to you. Pray for those who are cruel. . . . Luke 6:28-29*

Remember that Internet information is not always factual. Whether you're chatting or surfing Web sites, be skeptical about information and people. Not everything on the Internet is true. You don't have to be afraid of the Internet, but you should always be cautious. Practice caution with others even in Christian chat rooms.

It's okay to chat about your likes and dislikes, but *never* give out personal information. Do not tell anyone your name, phone number, address, or even the name of your school, team, church, or neighborhood. Be cautious. . . . *You will be like sheep among wolves. So be as smart as snakes. But also be like doves and do nothing wrong. Be careful of people. . . .Matthew 10:16-17*

STRANGER ONLINE

16/junior

e-name: faithful1

best friend: Maya

site area: Thought for the Day

Confident. Caring. Swimmer. Single-handedly built TodaysGirls.com Web site. Loves her folks. Big brother Ryan drives her nuts! Great friend. Got a problem? Go to Amber.

AMBER THOMAS

JAMIE CHANDLER

PORTRAIT OF LIES

15/sophmore

e-name: rembrandt

best friend: Bren

site area: Artist's Corner

Quiet. Talented artist. Works at the Gnosh Pit after school. Dad left when she was little. Helps her mom with younger sisters Jordan and Jessica. Babysits for Coach Short's kids.

ALEX DIAZ

TANGLED WEB

14/freshman

e-name: newkid

best friend: Morgan

site area: to be determined . . .

Spicy. Hot-tempered Texan. Lives with grandparents because of parents' problems. Won state in freestyle swimming at her old school. Snoops. Into everything. Break the rules.

R U 4 REAL?

16/junior
e-name: nycbutterfly
best friend: Amber
site area: What's Hot–What's Not
(under construction)

MAYA CROSS

Fashion freak. Health nut. Grew up in New York City.
Small town drives her crazy. Loves to dance.
Dad owns the Gnosh Pit. Little sis Morgan is also
a TodaysGirl.

BREN MICKLER

LUV@FIRST SITE

15/sophmore
e-name: chicChick
best friend: Jamie
site area: Smashin' Fashion

Funny. Popular. Outgoing. Spaz. Cheerleader. Always late.
Only child. Wealthy family. Bren is chatting–
about anything, online and off, except when
she's eating junk food.

CHAT FREAK

14/freshman
e-name: jellybean
best friend: Alex
site area: Feeling All Write (under construction)

MORGAN
CROSS

The Web-ster. Spends too much time online. Overalls.
M&Ms. Swim team. Tries to save the world. Close to her
family—when her big sister isn't bossing her around.

Net Acronyms

2 to/too

4 for

ACK! disgusted

A/S/L age/sex/location

B4 before

BBL be back later

BBS be back soon

BF boyfriend

BRB be right back

CU see you

Cuz because

CYAL8R see you later

Dunno don't know

Enuf enough

FYI for your information

G2G or GTG got to go

GF girlfriend

GR8 great

H&K hug and kiss

IC I see

IN2 into

IRL in real life

JLY Jesus loves you

JK just kidding

JMO just my opinion

K okay

Kewl cool

KOTC kiss on the cheek

LOL laugh out loud

LTNC long time no see

LY love you

L8R later

NBD no big deal

NU new/knew

NW no way

OIC oh, I see

QT cutie

RO rock on

ROFL rolling on floor laughing

RU are you

SOL sooner or later

Splain explain

SWAK sealed with a kiss

SYS see you soon

Thanx (or) thx thanks

TNT till next time

TTFN ta ta for now

TTYL talk to you later

U you

U NO you know

UD you'd (you would)

UR your/you're/you are

WB welcome back

WBS write back soon

WTG way to go

Y why

(Note: Remember that capitalization may vary.)